I0596325

THE TROUBLE WITH MR. PRETTY

SONIA STANIZZO

The Trouble with Mr. Pretty

Copyright © 2017, 2021 Sonia Stanizzo

First Published by Beachwalk Press: 2017

Second Edition: 2021

ISBN: 9780645090819

Publisher: JRL Publishing

Editor: Sassie Lewis

Cover: Outlined with Love Designs

No part of this book may be used or reproduced without written permission, except in the case of brief quotations in articles and reviews.

This book is a work of fiction and any resemblance to persons, living or dead, or places, events or locales is purely coincidental. The characters are productions of the author's imagination and used fictitiously.

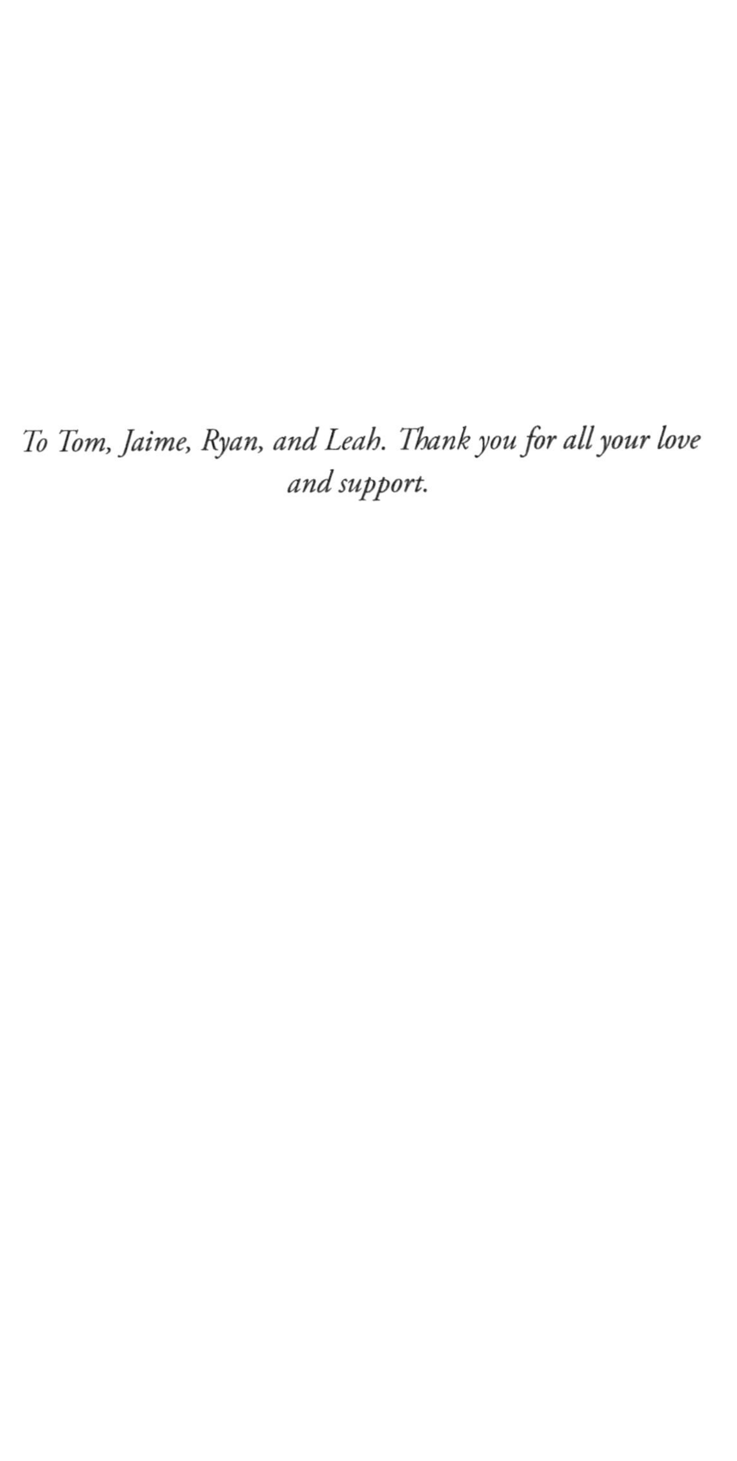

To Tom, Jaime, Ryan, and Leah. Thank you for all your love and support.

Chapter 1

*L*auren Moore swung the *closed* sign of her gift shop into place and glanced through the tinted glass. The street had been blocked, stopping vehicle access to the quaint shops in the seaside village, and now the street was beginning to fill up with rowdy people ready to celebrate the New Year. She smiled and made her way to the back of the shop, thankful she'd be gone before the crowds rolled in.

Post-Christmas trading had been the busiest in years, and Lauren had rung up the sale for the last customer only moments ago. Her legs ached from standing all day, and a headache pounded at her temples. She couldn't wait to go home, soak in the tub, then crawl into bed. She longed for the oblivion of sleep to block the memories of the worst New Year's Eve of her life.

She didn't want to remember that night; the pain always brutally crushed her heart.

Thunderous banging sounded behind her. Startled,

she swung around. A tall, silhouetted figure stood on the opposite side of the dark glass. Taking a few steps closer, she pointed at the sign.

The knocking grew louder and more persistent, then the man put his hands under his chin as if in prayer and mouthed *please*.

Feeling drained from the day, she sighed, slumped her shoulders, and pulled the keys out of her pocket. Then she made her way to the door and opened it. Would this day ever end?

On a gust of December heat the man barreled into her shop of dainty gifts, and did a quick scan of the area before stopping in front of a display of delicate tea sets. With his broad shoulders and chest, he looked too big to be anywhere near her pretty breakables. She needed to get him out fast.

"Is there something I can help you with?" She asked, her attention focused on the expensive teapot in his large, strong hands.

She breathed a sigh of relief when he set the fragile item back on the shelf before turning to face her. "You're a lifesaver for opening for me."

His crooked smile flashed white teeth and the force hit her like a lightning bolt to the chest. She drew in a sharp breath as heat rushed through her veins. The greenest eyes she'd ever seen surrounded by thick, dark eyelashes sparkled at her while faint creases fanned out from the corners. His dark brown hair was cut short at the sides of his head but kept longer on top. It looked tousled, like impatient fingers had ploughed through it. His faded denim jeans, stamped with a designer label, molded firmly around a tight rear end and muscular legs, something she'd gotten a brief glance at before he turned. A black shirt stretched across his broad shoulders, the top buttons open, giving her a peek of a strong chest.

The man was absolutely gorgeous, and the fact she noticed was shocking. Her best friends, Ava and Jade, often teased that if Channing Tatum walked past she wouldn't give him a second glance because Lauren no longer saw a pretty face...well, up until now. This man, and the pretty packaging he came in, couldn't be ignored, and she wondered why out of all the men who, according to her friends, were babes, did she notice this one? He looked vaguely familiar. She couldn't put her finger on where she might have seen him before, but she was positive he'd never been a customer.

Ava and Jade would freak if she told them she'd finally noticed a *Mr. Pretty*. Actually, keeping this unsettling discovery to herself was best. They'd start setting her up on blind dates again with all the pretty boys they knew. No, she couldn't put herself through that torture again. Those dates had been disastrous. They'd been good-looking men who couldn't see past their own attractive reflection. Although a part of her felt relieved that after all these years she'd finally noticed a handsome man; she wasn't broken after all...well, not completely.

"I need something to get myself out of big trouble," he finally answered. His deep voice sounded as smooth as whiskey.

Heat sizzled and stirred around her, making the room

feel like a sauna. Was the air conditioning off already? The need to get him out of the shop fast was crucial; otherwise, she feared she might melt into a steamy puddle at his feet.

"Does 'getting you out of big trouble' have a price tag?" she asked.

"After the mess I'm in, the sky's the limit." He grinned.

"A desperate man with lots to spend—you're my favorite customer," she joked, keeping it light while her insides turned to a quivering mush. "How much trouble are you in?"

One large shoulder shrugged as he dipped his head and dug his hands into the pockets of his jeans. "Enough for me to pound on your door after closing time."

The devilish smile showed he knew how to get himself out of all sorts of trouble. Why

did men think women could be appeased by a charming smile and expensive gifts? A stab of shame pierced Lauren's thoughts as she remembered a time when she could be won over by sparkly trinkets and a dazzling smile. She'd learned the hard way that shiny things soon tarnished.

She led him to a black velvet display. "We have beautiful lockets with intricate designs and some with lovely colored gems. What's your wife's style?"

"I'm not married."

"Your girlfriend?"

"It's for my mother," he clarified.

"Oh." She hadn't seen that coming. A get-out-of-trouble gift was usually for a lover.

Her friends had to constantly remind her that not all handsome men were scheming jerks with secret agendas, but she had yet to meet one. After her horrifying experience with Graham Stone, she never wanted to look at, or get involved with, another good-looking male ever again.

With stiff fingers, she touched the locket around her neck. It wasn't one of the pretty gem-encrusted ones she sold, but to her it was much more valuable. Lauren had found the cheap silver locket years ago at a small seaside market she'd been aimlessly walking through. A precious yet painful reminder lay locked inside. A big reminder of why she kept away from men who looked too good to be true.

Needing to focus on work, Lauren inwardly shook herself. Scanning the shop, she decided a vase might be more appropriate for his mother and moved closer to a display cabinet with a colorful array of crystals in all shapes and sizes.

"These are lovely if you think your mother would like them."

He ambled over to the cabinet, closing the distance between them. The smell of sunshine, sea breeze, and man surrounded her and sent her senses into overdrive. She clutched anxious fingers around her locket and stepped away, only for her back to press against the wall, giving her no more room to move.

As he looked inside the cabinet, oblivious to the

turmoil he was causing her, Lauren examined his profile. The start of an afternoon shadow covered a square jawline. His long, narrow nose had a small bump on the bridge, the only flaw on his chiseled face. He bit his lower lip as he studied the vases, and for a moment, she wondered how they would taste.

Where were these outrageous thoughts coming from?

Lauren desperately needed to put more space between them. Standing so close was making it impossible to think, but to move would involve brushing past him. Touching him wasn't going to help with her jumbled thoughts and sensations. She hadn't reacted to a man like this since Graham.

When she trusted her voice not to quiver, she excused herself. He stepped back, giving her room to pass, but not enough to avoid contact, and her bare arm brushed the length of his strong, firm one. Another blast of heat shot from him and into her. Blinking up at him, their gazes locked, and she searched those piercing green orbs to see if he'd felt it too. His emerald eyes held hers.

Unable to pull away from his penetrating gaze, she reached for the metal locket, but its coolness did nothing to remind her that being so close to this heat-missile was a bad idea.

A shrill tooting of horns outside broke the spell, and she glanced out the window. A bunch of excited New Year's Eve revelers, with colorful hats and party horns, crowded the footpath in front of the shop.

"They've started early," she said on a shaky breath, using the noisy distraction to move away from him. She scurried behind the counter, putting a safety barrier between them.

He flicked a glance over his shoulder at the partygoers. "It will be a great night for it."

By his casual stance she would have believed him unaffected by the burning moment they'd just shared, but heat still smoldered in his eyes. Then, in a blink of an eye, it was gone. Could she have imagined it? It had been so long since anyone had come even close to looking at her that way that she probably read the signs wrong.

Needing to get back to the reason he was there, and not be distracted by that liquid green heat, she cleared her throat. "Do you see anything you like?" She relaxed a little because her voice sounded professional and not like the trembling mess simmering on the inside.

The liquid heat was back in his eyes and they raked over her in a way that said *she* was what he liked. A sharp breath caught in her lungs and her heart began to race. Surely she didn't get *that* signal wrong?

"The vases…do you like any of them?" she managed to croak out.

His lips tilted in a knowing smile, like he knew she'd been rattled, then he sauntered closer, as if he had all the time in the world. "They're very nice, but her house is full of them. I recognize a couple in your display."

God, hurry up and pick something, then leave! The warm, relaxing bubble bath she planned for the evening would have to be replaced with a long, cold shower. "Do you have any idea what her tastes are?"

"I do know she loves this shop. She tells me she comes

here all the time. I think she's dropping hints for me to buy stuff from here."

"Looks like it worked. What's your mother's name? If she's a regular customer, I'd probably know who she is."

"Susan Henderson. I'm Jack." He stood there with his hand out.

The name froze her on the spot for a beat. Now she knew why he looked so familiar, but it wasn't because of a family resemblance to his mother. It was because Jade had been drooling over the man standing in Lauren's shop for over a decade. Until a couple of years ago, Jack had been the captain of Jade's favorite football team, The Flaming Stars. He was now retired due to an injury. Susan often spoke of her children but never mentioned she was the mother of a very famous football player. Lauren, who wasn't into sports or sport stars, never knew the two were related.

Jade also followed Jack off the football field and kept Lauren and Ava updated on his social life. Lauren refused to read gossip magazines since the day she had seen Graham's proud, beaming face staring back at her from the pages of one of them with the news that had shocked her life. But Jade loved reading them, and according to her, Jack had been involved with a string of women from actresses to supermodels and everything in between. Lauren always believed Jade exaggerated his infamous relationships. The media liked to embellish or even make stories up so they could sell their magazines. But after seeing Jack in the flesh and witnessing his charm, she could understand how women didn't stand a chance against him.

From the moment he charged into the shop he embodied confidence, charm, and beauty. His casual clothing did nothing to hide the quality and expense, nor did they hide the powerful body beneath them. Instincts screamed to keep her distance. Jack was definitely a *Mr. Pretty*. Mr. Pretty was a nickname Jade and Ava had made up when Lauren started keeping away from all attractive men, especially if they were also very successful.

Warning bells clanged *back away now*! If he weren't Susan's son, she would have quickly ushered him out the door, with or without a gift. But Susan was one of her best customers and someone whom she liked very much. Not only did Susan shop there often, she'd noticed Lauren's unique way of decorating the place and encouraged—more like insisted— Lauren to redecorate Susan's bedroom. The woman had been so happy with the results she passed on a good word to her friends. With another two bedrooms lined up for clients, Lauren was busy collecting the necessary pieces. It was very exciting that her business was branching out into design. A little scary too. She wasn't a qualified interior designer but people were trusting her with their homes.

Eyeing Jack's waiting hand like it was a snake ready to strike, she reluctantly accepted it. His large, firm grip smothered hers, and a jolt of heat zapped up her arm to slam into her chest.

Freezing for a beat, she finally managed to say, "I'm Lauren Moore. Susan told me about her inconsiderate son not making it home for Christmas. I assume this is why you're in her bad books?" She tried to sound amused.

"She's made no secret that she's not happy with me." He chuckled, keeping her hand in his strong grasp and showing no signs of letting go. Heat traveled at the speed of light through the rest of her body, warming her from head to toe.

The warning bells clanged louder, telling her to move slowly and carefully away from the imminent threat. With a light tug, she pulled her hand free and placed it on the counter's surface, hoping the cool stone would help bring her body temperature back to normal. It didn't work.

Focus. Lauren needed to focus, sell him something, and get him to leave. She didn't understand what the reaction to him was about. This was new to her. "I have a mirror in my office I put aside for her because she was looking for something to hang in her entryway. I'm sure she'll love it. Just give me a minute and I'll get it."

She hurried to the office, thankful for a few minutes alone to get her messed-up head and body back in order. Closing the door behind her, Lauren leaned back on it, shut her eyes, and took a deep breath. It helped with her shaking hands but did nothing to slow her racing heart.

There wasn't anything she could do about her heart rate so she picked up the French provincial style mirror leaning against the wall and glanced at her reflection. Bright pink spots flushed her cheeks and neck—the result of a mere brush of an arm and a touch of a hand. What was happening to her?

When her body settled down, allowing her to function normally, Lauren carried the mirror into the shop and placed it on the counter. "If Susan doesn't love it, she can always bring it back and exchange it for something else."

Jack flipped over the little white tag, revealing the price, and whistled. "My mother sure does have expensive taste."

Guilt gnawed at her for showing him such an expensive item. "I have candlesticks which are much cheaper, and I'm sure she'd like those too."

She started to pick the mirror up to take it back to her office, but he placed a hand on it, stopping her. "If I want to get back into her good books, I better make it great."

"Having you home will be enough for Susan. She doesn't need gifts."

"How she has you fooled." He chuckled.

His smooth laugh sent a shiver up and down her spine. Damn, she needed to get him out of the shop. The sooner the better.

Lauren carefully placed the mirror in a box, wrapped it up in pretty pink and white paper, and attached an elaborate pale blue bow in the corner. After ringing up the sale, she wished him luck with his mother and led him to the door.

"Thanks for opening for me." He held out his hand, and she had no other choice but to take it. A quick, feather-light stroke of his thumb brushing along her fingers had Lauren sucking in a soft gasp. *Did his gaze just drop to my lips?*

She let go of his hand as if burned by hot coals and

leaned past him to open the door, making every effort for their bodies not to touch.

He stepped onto the street filling up with partygoers and said, "Happy New Year, Lauren."

"Happy New Year, Jack." She quickly averted her gaze and closed the door with a resounding *click*.

Turning her back toward the man that had barreled into her shop and upset her senses, Lauren walked over to turn the lights off, but before she did, she took a moment to glance around the room. She was proud of her shop—Everything Nice—with its mixture of what she believed to be beautiful and feminine. She stocked everything from unique and unusual homewares, pictures, tea sets, and clocks to more personal items such as jewelry, perfumes, and lingerie.

Lauren began working at Everything Nice when she started university, then, two years ago, she bought the business from her boss and wonderful friend Lillian. When Lauren took over, it only needed a fresh coat of paint and a revamp of the tired-looking sign on the front window. Now, with Lauren's name on the paperwork, the responsibility of keeping it successful lay on her shoulders.

Lauren never thought she'd be a shop owner. She'd spent her first year at university studying to be a lawyer. Her job at Everything Nice was only meant to be temporary; something to help pay her uni fees. But her heart had never truly been satisfied with the career path she'd chosen. It had just been her way of showing her family how far she'd come without any help from them. But while working in the shop she'd discovered her creative side and her happy place. So when her life came crashing down hard in her second year of law school she didn't think twice about giving up her degree and working full-time with Lillian. If it weren't for Lillian and her shop, she didn't know where she'd be right now. She had Lillian, Ava, and Jade, to thank for keeping her from falling apart.

She was satisfied with her life now, and she didn't need some Mr. Pretty barging into it and upsetting everything. But hopefully she'd never see this Mr. Pretty again. Sighing, she turned the lights off and headed for home.

Chapter 2

Lauren pulled into her driveway to find Ava and Jade sitting on the little brick fence in front of the house she shared with Lillian. Grocery bags overflowing with enough food and alcohol for a dozen people sat by their feet.

Groaning her frustration, because she'd hoped for a quiet night alone, she blew out a long breath and got out of the car. The late afternoon sky had turned a deep orange, and a slight breeze played with the strands of hair around her face. Lauren folded her arms across her chest as she made her way over to them, silently praying there weren't more people hidden.

"You girls promised me you were going to some big New Year's Eve party this year," Lauren said.

Her two closest friends shared a guilty look between them. Even though neither one of them were currently involved, Lauren knew they wouldn't have any problem finding someone to share a New Year's kiss with. Ava was tall, dark, and exotic with sultry brown eyes and an olive complexion, while Jade was petite with a fiery mop of auburn hair and sparkling blue eyes.

"You are our big New Year's Eve party," Ava said with a mischievous look in her eyes.

"Please don't get mad," Jade said. "We know you didn't want to go out to a party, so we brought the party to you."

Darting her gaze past them, Lauren had a mental image of people jumping out from behind the bushes and yelling *Surprise!*

Jade must have sensed Lauren's distress and quickly added, "It's only us and plenty of junk food and wine."

"You told me you weren't going to babysit me this year. I had plans to soak in a hot bath and relax. I've had a busy week, and I'm tired. I'm not going to be very good company."

"Don't worry." Ava linked her arm through Lauren's, leaving Jade to collect the bags.

"You can have your bath and we'll bring the party into the bathroom while you soak."

Lauren shook her head and laughed. "Why did I think you would actually listen to me this year?"

"We will listen to you when you start talking sense." Ava pulled her up the stairs. "But for now, it's time to open a bottle of Merlot."

Lauren had opted for a quick shower instead of soaking in a hot tub. If she took too long, Ava would no doubt start the party in the bathroom.

Why did she think they'd leave her alone this New Year's Eve? They hadn't for the past eight years. It was Jade and Ava who'd helped pull her out of the darkest night of her life—the night she had lost her precious baby girl.

Lauren met the girls while attending the University of Sydney. Both her and Ava had been studying law, while Jade had been studying to be a primary school teacher. A solid and close friendship developed immediately. They were as close as sisters; in Lauren's case, closer.

She hadn't spoken to her older sister Belinda in months and was thankful for that.

A soft knock sounded before Jade popped her head around the bedroom door, concern creasing her brow. "Everything okay in here?"

Hanging her clothes on the back of the chair, Lauren nodded and tried to smile to reassure Jade, but the ache in her heart made it too difficult.

"Oh, Lauren." Jade sighed as she sat on the edge of the bed. "It kills me to see you so sad. What can I do to help?"

"Just being here is all the help I need." Lauren picked up Jade's hand and gave it a gentle squeeze.

Eight years ago she'd sat amongst a happy crowd of New Year's Eve revelers. A display of red, green, and gold fireworks had exploded above her head, falling like rain, but she never saw its brilliance. The people around her laughed, danced, kissed—and made promises they never intended to keep—but those things were as far away from Lauren as the stars in the sky.

Lauren had sat on a prickly patch of grass and waited for the pain to come. Wishing for it to consume her, wanting it to rip through her body with the force of a sledgehammer. Anything would've been better than the dull emptiness that had spread through her body like an evil disease. She'd wanted to cry, yell...grieve, but her body wouldn't do what her mind screamed for it to do.

Her *sisters* were her rock, and they always knew when Lauren needed them the most.

New Year's Eve was always one of those days.

Jade narrowed her eyes. "You don't have to pretend for us."

"I know. I'm fine, really. I'm ready to have a drink and unwind." She pointed toward the door. "You'd better get back out there before Ava drinks all the alcohol."

Jade laughed. "Don't worry, we brought enough to last until next New Year's Eve." She pushed herself up from the bed. "But I better go and supervise just in case."

Lauren gave Jade a quick hug and whispered, "Thank you."

"Anytime," Jade said, giving her a squeeze.

After she left Lauren pulled out a small, wooden box from her chest of drawers. It contained a small, soft beanie, a baby pink wrap covered with butterflies, and an ultrasound photo. Lauren picked up the fuzzy black-and-white picture, its edges worn from being held so many times, and looked at the precious baby she'd lost. Eight years ago to the day she'd given birth to a stillborn baby girl, but the gut-wrenching pain and sadness still smothered her and tore at her heart like it happened only yesterday. She had wanted to give her daughter all the love and attention a child deserved. Everything her own mother never gave her.

When Lauren was born, her father left before her first nappy had even been changed, and her mother, Dorothy, blamed his departure on Lauren. Dorothy was either passed out or too drunk to ever show Lauren any kind of affection. There had been no loving kisses before bedtime and no soothing cuddles after waking from a bad dream. She never asked about her day at school nor was she interested in anything Lauren achieved. Not once did she tell Lauren she loved her.

The day Lauren found out she was pregnant, she made the stupid decision of telling her mother and sister, hoping that for once in her life she'd get some support. She was nineteen and needed them. Instead of help and support, Belinda laughed so hard tears streamed down her face, while telling Lauren she'd lived up to being the big slut she always knew she was. Lauren had never understood why her sister had been so hostile toward her. It was most likely Dorothy's damaging influence.

Dorothy had flopped down on the threadbare, stain-covered sofa, lit a cigarette, and told her she didn't want a screaming brat living in the house. That she wanted Lauren gone before the thing was born. Lauren hadn't waited; that same day she packed up her few measly belongings and left the run-down house of misery and the people living in it. They were never truly a family and never would be. She'd run straight to Ava, Jade, then Lillian, who let her move into the apartment above her garage. Lillian became the loving mother she'd never had and Ava and Jade her loyal sisters. Their blood may not run through her veins, but these were the people she would die for.

Lauren gently kissed the photo, and with one last loving look, placed it back in the box, wondering if the pain would ever fade.

It was time to join her friends. She couldn't stay in her room all night. Though Lauren knew if she wanted to sit and cry, they would cry with her. If she wanted to be cheered up, they would be the clowns. Or if she wanted to get plastered so she didn't have to think at all, they would pass her the bottle. But she'd had enough of crying. She wanted to enjoy the company of her beautiful friends and for once celebrate the New Year.

Empty bottles and packets of chips littered Lauren's glass coffee table as the three women sat around drinking and laughing long after the clock struck midnight. The new year had begun and they hadn't noticed. They'd finished their fourth bottle of Merlot and where now into the Midori and pineapple juice.

Ava tucked her feet up on the sofa and pointed a wobbly finger at Lauren and Jade. Tonight she had dressed in figure-hugging black jeans and a cherry red crop top. Her silky, black, chin-length hair, which she'd tucked behind a diamond-studded ear, didn't have a strand out of place. Ava always looked immaculate everywhere she went. Even drunk, she couldn't look disheveled if she tried. "Do you realize that I haven't had a boyfriend in years?" Ava asked.

"Not that I'm complaining—who wants to have the same guy in your life every day?"

Jade rolled her eyes. "Ava, you've had too much to drink. You've had heaps of boyfriends. It was only last week you were sleeping with…with…what was his name?" She tapped the side of her head with her index finger like it would somehow improve her memory.

Auburn curls sprung loose from a hair clip and bounced uncontrollably around her face. Unlike Ava's immaculate appearance, Jade's floral, long skirt was rumpled, and her top was pulled out from the waistband of the skirt.

"Greg," supplied Lauren at the same time Jade pointed a finger in the air and said, "Aha! Fred!"

Ava scoffed. "It was Bill. Greg was last month, and I've *never* slept with anyone named Fred."

"Then who's Fred?" Jade scratched her head, looking baffled. Then her eyes lit up as she remembered. "Francis from my yoga class is sleeping with Fred."

Lauren and Ava sank into the cushions of the couch in a fit of giggles.

When Ava caught her breath she said, "Bill was never my boyfriend. We only went out a couple of times, and he wasn't any good, so I told him I was going to be busy for a while."

Ava's idea of *going out* was drinks and sex at her place, or his, or the bathroom at the bar they were at. And if she said he wasn't *any good* she meant the sex had been *really* bad.

"I'm surprised you gave him more than one chance," Lauren said.

"Oh, he was sooo cute, just looking at his face was worth the bad sex," Ava said, her words slurring.

Shaking a finger at Ava like she was a naughty girl, Lauren said, "I've told you hundreds of times never, ever, ever get fooled by a pretty face. Don't you listen to me? They are no good. You need to keep far, far away." She picked up her glass and swallowed the remainder of the sweet liquid. "I saw a pretty face today, actually a really hot face. He bought a super-expensive mirror for his mother, but do you see me falling into bed with him? Noooo. He's a snake. I know to keep away from Mr. Pretty." With that she nodded, making her head spin. She pulled her shoulders back and puffed her chest out, pleased that she had resisted the temptation.

Her friends stared at her with their eyes wide and their mouths dropped open. "You noticed a Mr. Pretty?" Jade finally asked.

Lauren realized the mistake she'd made and stuffed her mouth full of potato chips so she couldn't answer.

Stumbling over to Lauren, Jade sat on the other side of her and put a palm on Lauren's forehead. Lauren swatted the hand away like it was a pesky fly, managing to slap her own face in the process.

"She must be sick." Jade turned to Ava, looking

concerned. "She noticed a Mr. Pretty. That never happens."

Ava picked up Lauren's wrist and put her fingers on her pulse. "Hmm, her heart rate's a little fast. This Mr. Pretty is getting her very excited."

With a sharp tug, Lauren pulled free from Ava's grip. "I knew I shouldn't have told you." She frowned at the empty glass in her hand, banged it back down on the coffee table, and pointed an accusing finger at it. "That's what made me tell you. I can't keep anything to myself when I drink more than I should." She threw a dirty look at the glass.

"So how pretty was he?" Excitement lit Jade's face.

"What would you rate him out of ten?" Ava asked.

Lauren swiveled her head from left to right to look at them. Feeling dizzy from watching them like a tennis match, she covered her eyes. Dammit, she wanted her friends to stop asking questions.

Ava removed Lauren's hands from her heated face. "You have to tell us. Spill. Now."

They were determined to get this out of her, so the quicker she got it over with, the better. "He was more than a ten. So he was *extremely* pretty. There, happy now? I don't want to talk about this anymore. I want nothing to do with Mr. Pretty, so don't make a big deal out of it, okay?"

"No, it's not okay! And yes, it is a big deal." Jade's voice rose. "Well, when it's been…I don't know…eight years since you've noticed one, I'd say it's a major deal, and since you've never taken notice before, this might mean something."

Lauren shook her head. "Nope, means nothin'." She hiccupped. "Not one little thing." She put her hands on Jade and Ava's knees and pushed up onto legs that wobbled like jelly. "I need to pee."

And with that she made her way into the bathroom, hoping the tight feeling in her belly was the result of too much wine and not because *Mr. Pretty* was still having an unsettling effect on her.

Chapter 3

The smells of roasting meat and baked vegetables surrounded Jack as he entered his mother's kitchen. His mouth watered, and his stomach grumbled. Jack knew how to slap a few things together to get by, but the alluring smells reminded him of how much he missed his mother's cooking.

"Hey, Mum, smells great in here. Is Dad home?"

Pausing at the stove, she glanced over her shoulder. "No, I sent him out to buy wine, and it's about time you came home."

Her voice sounded stern, but the glimmer in her eyes couldn't hide how happy she was to see him. At fifty-six his mother looked like she was only just entering her forties. Light brown hair fell in gentle waves and brushed the tops of her shoulders. The emerald green wrap-around dress she wore highlighted her green eyes, a feature Jack had inherited.

"I've missed you. Is that a new dress? You look amazing." He placed the mirror on the kitchen counter, wrapped his arms around her, and kissed her cheek.

"Flattering me will not make me forget you missed Christmas. Christmas, Jack! The family is always together for Christmas. And you missed Emma's first one too...she was very upset."

"Emma is four weeks old, the only thing she gets upset about is if she's crapped herself." He laughed.

With a sigh, his mother placed her hands on her hips. "Well, Leah knows, and she's not happy with you either."

A shipment of sneakers sponsored by America's newest tennis sensation, Leo Baker, sitting in a warehouse waiting to be unpacked was the reason he hadn't made it home in time for Christmas—that, and a severe snowstorm had blown in while he was finishing up his business in the US. When his sister Leah saw the personally signed sneakers from Leo that Jack had left for her in the living room she wouldn't stay mad for long.

Kissing his mother's cheek again, he said, "I'm here for New Year's, but I've had a lot of invites to fantastic parties tonight, so if you're not happy to see me…" He flicked his wrist out and checked the time on his watch. "I might make it in time."

Giving him a playful slap on the arm, she said, "You're not going anywhere." Then her gaze flicked to the package on the counter. "What's that?"

"Knew it wouldn't take you long to notice that. It's your Christmas present."

"Did you think you could buy your way out of trouble?" She frowned.

"That was the plan," he answered, unabashed.

The frown turned into a smile as she unwrapped the gift with as much excitement as a kid on Christmas morning. She gasped and looked at him with wide eyes. "Jack, it's beautiful. It looks like something from the shop I love."

He leaned a hip against the kitchen counter. "It is."

"How do you know about that shop?"

"You keep raving about the one on Marshall Street and dropping major hints about it."

"I do not drop hints," she said with exasperation.

"Yeah, you do." Then he explained how he nearly had to break the door down to get inside.

"I'm sure you would have impressed Lauren." She grimaced as she examined the mirror.

"She was more than happy to help me out." Actually, she'd scurried around the shop like she couldn't wait to get him out of there fast enough. She probably had some big New Year's Eve party to get to.

"Hmm." His mother didn't look convinced. "I like Lauren's shop, but I like her even more. I hope you didn't leave a bad impression. I don't want her to think my family is rude."

"Don't worry. I made a great impression. I had her eating out of my hand," he joked, but a smidgen of doubt crept in. He wasn't so sure he had.

"I roughly know the price of a mirror like this. I'd say she had *you* eating out of her hand." She kissed Jack's cheek. "I love it. Thank you. You know it's you I wanted home, you didn't need to buy me an expensive gift."

"That's exactly what Lauren said. I wish I'd listened, I could have saved myself a lot of cash."

"Lauren's a smart girl and absolutely lovely."

Lovely wouldn't be how he'd describe her. When he entered Lauren's shop he thought he'd walked into the wrong place. She looked more like someone who should be posing for a modeling shoot not working in a gift shop. Sexy, honey-blonde hair had been pulled back into a high ponytail that hung past slender shoulders. Bright hazel eyes with golden flecks were surrounded with long, thick eyelashes. Her finely boned face smiled at him with full, lush, glossy lips with a hint of annoyance for having to re-open. And if her face wasn't incredible enough, her tall, sinewy body made his mouth water.

"Do you know if she's seeing anyone?" he asked casually.

"Forget it. You're not her type." She glanced over her shoulder at him as she bustled around the kitchen checking on dinner.

"What do you mean I'm not her type? And how do you know what her type is anyway?"

"A while back I had a chat with her assistant Jaime—another sweet girl, loves a good chat—about whether Lauren was seeing anyone."

Folding his arms across his chest, he asked, "Now why would you be interested if she was seeing anyone?"

Ducking her head, avoiding his gaze, she shrugged. "Curiosity?"

"Mum…" Jack pushed away from the counter and

stood in front of her, forcing her to look up at him. "Why were you 'curious'?"

"Can't a mother find prospects for her son?" Huffing, she quickly stepped away from him, and checked on something boiling inside a pot.

His mother the *matchmaker*.

Wanting to help find him a suitable 'wife', she had a habit of setting him up with women she believed were appropriate candidates. He didn't need help in that department. Finding his own women had never been a problem, but if it was, his mother would be the last person he'd ask for help. Their opinion differed on the type of women he should date. A wedding and children was what she hoped for, but quick and easy flings, with no strings attached, was all he wanted. But lately, that didn't hold the same thrilling appeal it once did.

Usually, his mother enquiring about Lauren as a prospect would have annoyed him. He'd often told his mother to stay out of his love life, but Lauren sparked his interest, so this time he'd let her off.

"Why do you think I'm not Lauren's type?"

"Jaime told me Lauren doesn't go for anyone good-looking." She patted his cheek. "And you, my beautiful boy, are too good-looking."

He frowned. "Thanks for clearing that up."

Jack had retired three years ago from professional football, but he still maintained his strong, muscular shape. Running every morning and lifting weights three or four times a week kept him fit. He wasn't going to get fat like so many players did after they retired. And apart from a broken nose, his face had been spared from the hard knocks footy offered. His teammates joked about how he wasn't ugly enough for footy, and the media had dubbed him the *pretty boy* of rugby league. No matter how hard he hit in the game or how rough he played he could never shake the name off.

The broken nose actually hadn't happened on the footy field. It was the result of a sibling battle. When they were kids, Leah—his sister—in a fit of rage, because he'd chopped off all the hair from her favorite Barbie doll, threw her skateboard at his head. Her aim had been perfect, smacking him right in the nose. But if anyone asked, he claimed he broke it going into a tackle while playing for Brimdale Black.

The dish his mother pulled from the oven and placed on the counter filled the kitchen with the smell of rosemary and garlic. Removing her oven mitts, she said, "Don't take it personally, darling. Like I said, Lauren never goes out with anyone good-looking. Apparently, she doesn't even notice them."

There was no doubt that she'd noticed him. A man knew when a woman was interested. Jack had experienced it many times. But what he'd never experienced before was a woman trying to pretend the air didn't sizzle between them. Her breath had quickened and her nipples had peaked through the thin fabric of her white top. Yes, he'd helped himself to a good look. The signs of interest had flashed like a neon light from Lauren.

"I saw her out one time with a man who looked

rather..." She glanced around the kitchen as if searching for the right word. "Eccentric."

"Eccentric?" Jack repeated.

"Very intelligent-looking, unusually dressed." She shrugged.

"Sounds like a nerd."

"Jack!" she scolded like he was ten years old. "That's not nice, he looked…interesting."

"Why would she go out with guys who look 'interesting' when she's so hot?"

A frown creased her brow. "Looks aren't everything. Maybe she can look deeper than what's on the outside."

Do people like that really exist? The women he dated either wanted his money or liked

the fame and attention they got while dating a famous football player.

A noise coming from the front of the house stopped all conversation. Leah and her husband James had arrived, and they entered the kitchen, Leah cradling Emma in her arms.

"Hi, Ma. Where's Dad?" Leah kissed their mother's cheek. The resemblance between mother and daughter was strong. They shared the same bright green eyes and light brown hair— only Leah wore hers longer and straighter. Their bodies were petite and slender with the top of their heads only reaching Jack's shoulders.

"At the bottle shop. He'll be back soon." Taking Emma from Leah's arms, she cooed, "How's my beautiful baby?"

"Hello, my inconsiderate brother." Leah punched Jack in the arm.

"I totally planned a snowstorm," he grumbled. "Your signed Leo Baker sneakers are in the living room," he added with a soft punch back.

Leah clapped her hands excitedly and kissed him on the cheek. "You're forgiven."

Jack rolled his eyes. "Thank you," he said sarcastically.

"How are you, Jack?" James, who was a lot shorter than Jack with thinning salt-andpepper hair, shook his hand. "Everything go all right?"

In addition to being Jack's brother-in-law, James was the accountant for Henderson's Sports. The store sold everything from sportswear to the latest workout equipment. After retiring from football, Jack took over the business from his father when he'd fallen ill. When his father had recuperated, he sold the business to Jack so he could spend more time traveling with his wife. With Jack's big visions for the store, Henderson's was now opened in five major cities around Australia.

"Yeah, everything went well. The sneakers turned out great. I'm going to wait until after the Christmas sales to put them on the shelves," Jack said.

"They'll sell fast," James predicted.

"I'm expecting them to. The shops are going to be busy with orders. Leah needs to hurry up and finish her holiday and get her ass back to work, maybe the orders won't fall behind."

Leah, who was standing by their mother, fussing over Emma, stopped to glare at Jack.

"Hey, I'm on maternity leave, not *holiday*. I'm entitled to time off."

"Yeah, yeah. Just don't take too long."

"Isn't your new assistant working out?" she asked, concern lining her face.

"Yeah, she was great." Sarcasm laced his words.

Jack had hired Claire as his new assistant when Leah started maternity leave. He'd been so busy with the new stores opening he never had the time to check out her resumé references. Never would he admit to anyone that her sexy, curvaceous body, smoky gray eyes, and luscious chestnut-colored hair had swayed him into hiring her. Luckily, she'd worked hard and took initiative and soon had the office running smoothly. They worked closely together and he became aware of the light, casual flirting, the occasional brush of a hand on his arm, and the lowcut tops she began to wear.

One Friday night, a couple of days before leaving for the US, Jack had decided to enjoy a scotch in the office after work. It had been a hectic week, and he needed to unwind before going home. Claire had entered the office to ask if there was anything more she could do before leaving for the day. Not having any more work for her, she'd lingered for a few minutes, asking him about his plans for the weekend.

It hadn't been his intention for it to go any further than talking. He couldn't even blame it on the scotch— his mind had been crystal clear. An attractive, willing woman had offered herself to him and he happily accepted without thinking twice. Why not? Women in his social circle wanted him for just sex all the time. But Claire wasn't in his circle; she'd been his employee, and he should have known better and not followed through.

The moment it was over the ramifications hit. When he'd tried to apologize, telling her it should never have happened Claire had taken it badly. She responded by throwing a crystal paperweight at his head which, thankfully, missed and hit the wall behind him, smashing into tiny pieces.

When she screamed *I thought you loved me*, it shocked him more than the paperweight aimed at his head. Then she preceded to call him every derogative name he'd ever heard and some he hadn't, and promised to make his life a living hell before storming out of the office, cursing his name and slamming doors on the way out.

Dammit, he could kick himself for being so reckless. He wasn't dealing with football groupies anymore. He hoped that was the last he'd ever see of her, but he couldn't shake the bad feeling in the pit of his stomach.

"What happened?" Leah asked.

"Let's just say she didn't work out." He scowled at the memory.

With a knowing laugh, she said, "You are too good-looking for your own good. Unless it was only your money she was after, then your handsome face was just a bonus." Leah pulled a face when he tried to give her a threatening stare. "Don't worry. I'll be in for a couple of hours next week, but that's all I can do."

Throwing his hands in the air in mock frustration, he

grumbled, "Why on earth did I ever think having family work for me would be a good idea?"

Giving him a tight hug, she chuckled. "It's the best decision you've ever made, and you'd be lost without me."

He ruffled Leah's hair, because he knew it annoyed the crap out of her. He would never admit she was right. "Mum, hand over my niece. You're not going to hog her all night. You women have food to cook."

Jack ducked to avoid the kitchen utensils thrown at his head.

Chapter 4

Tuesday nights at Jovi's Pub had a quiet atmosphere. Soft jukebox music playing in the background replaced ear-splitting bands and rowdy weekend crowds. It was a place where the after-five work crowd could enjoy a relaxing drink. Lauren entered the pub through the heavy cedar doors with the name etched into the worn timber. The smell of beer and sweet alcohol wafted in the air.

She spotted Jade, a bright ball of bouncing energy fidgeting in her seat like a restless toddler. Her flaming red hair looked as hot as the desert sun. The bun tied unsuccessfully low on her head left uncontrollable strands springing around her face.

"Hey. Sorry I'm late," Lauren said as she slid onto the worn green vinyl seat opposite Jade and let out a long sigh. It had been a busy day, and she was happy to finally get off her tired feet.

"Compared to Ava, you're early." Jade looked at her watch. "She called from work, said she'll be here soon."

They met at Jovi's every Tuesday night for drinks. No other plans were ever made on this night. They'd been meeting there for the past three years, ever since Jade enrolled them in a Zumba class promising to be loads of fun. When they showed up for their lesson, the dance studio had been filled with a group of senior citizens. The older men's eyes bugged out of their heads and their faces flushed an unnatural shade of red as they took in the girl's tight, skin-baring gym gear. The girls ran out of the class before they gave someone a heart attack and drove to the nearest pub—Jovi's. And they'd been meeting there ever since.

Ava didn't keep them waiting long and arrived on a breeze of Chanel No. 5. She was dressed in a conservative navy business suit with a light blue scarf arranged around her neck. Her nondescript clothes, although well-tailored and of excellent quality, should have made her look plain and boring, but the suit couldn't hide her amazing body. Ava looked more like a *Sports Illustrated* model than a family law solicitor.

"Sorry I'm late." She blew Lauren and Jade air kisses, then picked up the drinks menu. "I got held up at work because my client is insisting she wants to keep the twelve-piece Royal Doulton dinner set she was given as a wedding gift."

Lauren and Jade exchanged confused looks.

Before Ava could explain, a young waiter rushed to their table to take their orders.

"Margaritas all around please." Ava beamed a stunning smile at him.

He fumbled the pencil in his fingers, catching it before it landed on the floor, then hurried away to get their drinks. Ava always had that effect on the opposite sex.

Ava slapped the menu on the table. "The dinner set was a wedding gift from her husband's mother and has been in his family for sixty years. So of course her husband wants it back, but she's refusing to hand it over." Pointing a manicured finger at them both, she went on. "If either of you are stupid enough to get married, you better come to me first. I'll set you up with an ironclad pre-nup."

"You don't have to worry about me getting married." Jade sighed, placed her elbows on the table, and propped her chin on her hands.

"Jade, you have to stop believing in that stupid curse," Lauren said. "You know it's a load of rubbish."

"It's not rubbish. It's true! My mother and sisters are proof. The Brennan women are cursed."

"You've had some bad luck—"

"The men in my family always leave. Hundreds of years ago, some witch in Ireland cursed our family so we can never find true love," she stated.

They paused in their conversation while the waiter returned with their drinks. Lauren hoped Ava didn't do anything to make him fumble again. She'd like to drink her margarita, not wear it.

When he left, without a drop spilled, Ava said, "Do

you know how crazy that sounds? Jade, trust me. Men leave their wives all the time. I see it every day. Anyway, you'll be better off not getting married. It will only cost you a mega amount of heartache and money."

"Ava!" Lauren scolded. "Just because you don't believe in marriage doesn't mean everyone should avoid it."

Ava shrugged an eloquent shoulder and said, "You probably won't get married either."

Lauren stared at Ava with surprise. "Why do you say that?"

"We've seen the few guys you've dated in the past—"

"So?"

"They're all losers," Ava said with no remorse.

Rolling her eyes, Lauren sighed. "Don't start with this again. There is nothing wrong with the guys I date."

Ava arched a dark eyebrow. "How long has it been since you've gone on a date anyway?"

Jumping in before Lauren could answer, Jade offered the information. "Eight months, that's how long it's been. The real question is how long has it been since you've had sex?"

Lauren fidgeted with the locket around her neck. She didn't want to be having this conversation. "Would you both mind your own business? I don't ask about your sex lives."

"That's because I *tell* you about mine." Ava smirked.

Lauren turned to Jade, desperately hoping for a change of subject, only to be ignored.

"It's been two years since you've had sex," Jade said. "And I don't think that the PeeWee Herman look-alike you were dating back then really counts. I seriously doubt he would have known what he was doing."

"He wasn't that bad," Lauren said with a shake of her head.

"Honey, if you say a man wasn't *that bad*, he definitely isn't doing it right. A man should be extraordinary. Curl-your-toes kind of extraordinary," Ava said.

"Oh my God!" Jade gasped.

"Yes, it should be *oh my God* worthy," Ava added.

Jade slowly shook her head. "No, not about that, I mean yes, it should be *oh my God* worthy, but I can't believe who just walked into Jovi's."

"Who?" Lauren and Ava both asked as they turned to look in the direction Jade was staring wide-eyed at.

A couple entered the pub and made their way to the empty stools arranged haphazardly around the carved wooden bar. Lauren's breath hitched, and a nervous flutter grew in her belly.

She knew exactly who had gotten Jade so excited.

Jack Henderson sat on a bar stool, looking even more handsome than he had on New Year's Eve—if that was possible. She had thought it was likely that she'd built him up to be better looking than he really was. But seeing him again, dressed in tight, faded jeans and a navy t-shirt, looking hotter than a man had the right to, told her that the pictures in her mind didn't do him justice.

Lauren's gaze darted to the woman sitting next to Jack. The black-haired beauty with a mass of tumbling, curly hair was dressed in a figure-hugging red dress show-casing a tanned, curvaceous body. She placed a hand on

Jack's toned arm and laughed with scarlet lips at something he'd said.

Dropping her gaze to her own hands, Lauren's heartbeat shuddered at an irregular pace. She didn't care that he was on a date and refused to let her treacherous heart tell her anything different.

"Go say hi." She heard Ava encourage Jade.

"No… I couldn't," she squeaked.

"Why not?" Ava asked.

"I can't just go to him and say hi. He's on a date."

Ava scoffed. "You're just saying hi."

Jade's eyes grew as round as saucers. She latched onto Lauren's wrist, digging sharp nails deep into the skin. "Oh my God, he's looking this way."

Lauren inwardly groaned. She tilted her head so her hair fell slightly over the side of her face and hoped Jack wouldn't see her. Although, they had only met once, so what were the chances of him remembering her? Especially when he had the Amazonian queen keeping him company.

The grip on Lauren's wrist tightened, and she was sure she'd be left with deep puncture wounds. "He's coming this way!"

The nearest exit was too far away to make a quick getaway before Jack arrived at their table.

"Hello, Lauren. I thought I recognized you. Ladies." He nodded at Ava and Jade.

Not wanting to be rude, Lauren plastered a smile on her face. "Jack, it's good to see you," she lied through her teeth. He made her heart and stomach do unfamiliar things, and she didn't like it one bit.

Jade's grip on her arm slackened, and Lauren glanced at her friends and watched as their jaws dropped open. They stared at her with a hundred questions burning in their eyes, and she knew she was in big trouble.

A moment of awkwardness passed before Lauren remembered her manners. "Jack, these are my friends Jade and Ava." She then pointed to Jade and added, "Jade's a huge fan of the Flaming Stars."

Jack beamed a smile in Jade's direction. "The Stars are looking good. They should have a great season this year."

Jade's face flushed as red as her hair, and she sat frozen with her mouth gapping. Then Lauren noticed her flinch, and she assumed Ava had kicked her under the table.

"Y–yes," she stuttered. "I've already bought my season tickets." Jack's low, sexy chuckle caused Lauren's belly to do a somersault.

"You really are a fan," he said.

Recovering from her frozen state, Jade giggled. Lauren saw Ava pinch the bridge of her nose and shake her head. Their friend was acting like a star-struck teenager. This time Lauren wanted to kick her.

Jack brought his attention back to Lauren. "The mirror was a huge hit. You were right though, she really only wanted me home." Jack's sexy smile had her burning up in the chair.

Picking up the drinks menu, she fanned it in front of her face, annoyed that his sexy smile and smooth-as-honey voice had her thinking about asking him back to her place so they could get naked. And that went against everything she believed in. She wanted to kick herself for reacting this way.

"That's great." Her voice sounded sharp.

Lauren hadn't meant to sound rude. Especially since she shouldn't have cared that he turned up the wattage of his sexy smile while flashing it at Jade. Lauren was supposed to be immune to men like Jack. There should have been no effect on her at all. But his masculinity, good looks, and his sex-on-legs demeanor were more powerful than anything she'd ever experienced.

Underneath the glitzy wrapping was a hot-blooded male who knew his way around a lot of women, and she needed to remember that. A prickling sensation at the back of her neck reminded her not to be tempted by the man and all that pretty packaging.

Just because she was angry with herself for forgetting her no *Mr. Pretty* policy, it didn't mean she had to be rude. She put the menu back down, mustered up a polite smile, and said,

"I'm glad you're back in Susan's good books."

"I'm sure it won't take me long to get out of it again." He laughed.

Jack placed a hand on the back of Lauren's chair and the tips of his warm fingers brushed along her bare shoulders. Thousands of goose bumps broke out over her skin and heat pooled down low. A shiver passed through her, and for a moment she had difficulty catching her breath. What was wrong with her?

"You know where my shop is if you get back into

trouble." She meant to sound happy to do business with him again, but instead, it sounded like she just wanted to see him.

Jack seemed to think so too, because his eyes lit up at the invitation. "I'll have to figure out a way to piss my mother off soon then."

After an awkward beat of silence, Ava, with a sultry lilt to her voice, purred, "So, Jack…" She draped her arm on the back of the chair, causing the fabric of her shirt to pull across a chest that most men couldn't ignore. "You look like you're still in good shape for someone who hasn't played football in a while." She leaned across the table and caressed a hand along his arm. "How do you keep so fit?"

Jack's voice was low with laughter. "I'm nowhere near as fit as I once was, but I do still like to run and do weights when I can."

"Where do you work out? I'm always looking for a gym partner."

Lauren clenched her jaw and fisted her hands in her lap, keeping them under the table in fear she might wrap them around Ava's pretty little neck. How dare she flirt with Jack? Didn't she have enough men to prey on without taking Jack from… No, he wasn't Lauren's. Ava had every right to flirt and do whatever she wanted to do with Jack. Lauren glanced over at Jade who also looked ready to kill Ava.

"I don't go to the gym. I have equipment at my office."

Ava sat back in her chair and pouted prettily. "That's a shame."

Jack glanced at Lauren and smiled. "Well, I better get back. It was great seeing you again." His fingers once again brushed against her bare shoulder as he stepped away. The touch sent an electric current blasting through her, almost short-circuiting her brain.

Then he turned and spoke to Jade and Ava. She didn't hear what he said because of the buzzing in her ears, but whatever it was it made Jade blush and Ava laugh.

The three women stared as he zigzagged his way through the tables and back to his date, giving them a great view of his toned backside in tight blue jeans.

Then Jade screeched loudly, causing Lauren to jump in the seat, breaking her mesmerized stare. "*That* was your Mr. Pretty? You didn't think to mention, especially to me, who has been following the Flaming Stars for years, that you met my favorite footy player?"

"I'm sorry." Lauren shrugged. She had wanted to forget meeting Jack, and not mentioning it to them was a good way of handling that. But one too many drinks had her spilling the beans about noticing a Mr. Pretty. They would have absolutely lost their minds if she'd told them *Mr. Pretty* was Jack Henderson.

Folding her arms across her chest, Jade shook her head, triggering more wild curls to spring free from the messy bun. "And you..." Eyes as sharp as lasers aimed at Ava. "Why were you flirting with Lauren's Mr. Pretty?"

Yes, Ava, why were you flirting with my Mr. Pretty? Lauren wanted to ask but kept her lips tightly sealed.

Ava stroked a finger around the rim of the margarita glass and licked the salty crystals off the tip. "It was a test.

I wanted to know his intentions toward Lauren. I had my boobs out for him to have a good ol' look, but his gorgeous green eyes never dropped for a second. Jack passed with flying colors, and he's totally hot for you, Lauren." At Jade's quick intake of breath, Ava added, "Sorry, Jade, but your sexy football player only had eyes for Lauren. I'd bet my next paycheck he was mentally strip searching her, and maybe even had the handcuffs ready."

Sagging with defeat in the chair, Jade put her elbow on the table and dropped her head in her hands. "I know." She gave a heavy sigh, then said, "He's all yours, Lauren."

Shocked by Ava's *test* and Jade's submission, Lauren's reply sounded strangled. "Did I miss something? Jack spoke to all of us." *And Ava even copped a feel.*

"I could feel the sexual tension between you two, even though Ava tried to get him to come over to the dark side. There's no denying it, *Mr. Pretty* is definitely yours, and I won't stand in the way." Jade sounded dejected.

At any other time Lauren would have found Jade's comment extremely amusing, but she was still reeling from the aftereffects of Jack's gentle touch on her shoulder and from her friends ridiculous reactions to her and Jack. "In case you haven't noticed, Jack is here with another woman."

Three heads turned toward the black-haired beauty sitting close to Jack. They both sat with drinks in hand, watching football on TV. Lauren hated everything Jack represented— money, fame, and looks. She'd learned the hard way that a pretty exterior could hide an ugly soul.

Ava turned her attention back to Lauren. "They both look more interested in what's on TV. I say go for it, Lauren."

"I'm not interested."

Jade shook herself from her sulk and let out an exaggerated sigh. "This is the first man you've noticed in eight years." When Lauren opened her mouth to argue Jade lifted a finger and stopped her. "Those Pee-Wee Herman guys don't count. I'm giving you my permission to take it further. Mr. Pretty is all yours." She slumped into her chair, looking miserable.

For a moment they sat quietly in their own thoughts. The jukebox playing an old Chicago ballad filled the silence.

Then Lauren's shoulders began to bop up and down. She bit her lip to stop them from twitching, but she couldn't help the peals of laughter escaping. Ava's laughter soon followed.

"Oh, Jade." Picking up a cocktail napkin, Lauren dabbed her eyes. "I'm so grateful that you're handing over *your* Mr. Pretty. Really I am," she said as Jade's eyes narrowed. Poor Jade didn't look happy about being laughed at, so Lauren cleared her throat and tried to keep a straight face. "Jack only came into the shop to buy a gift. That's all. Nothing more will ever happen."

"Sure." Jade sulked like a two-year-old.

Ava smiled like she knew a juicy secret.

Lauren's mirth died, and she blew out a frustrated

breath. Jade and Ava could be so stubborn. She hoped in a few days they'd forget all about Jack Henderson and leave her alone.

And pigs might fly.

Soon the waiter returned to their table, balancing a tray of margaritas, and placed a glass on the table in front of each woman. "Compliments of Mr. Henderson," he announced.

Jade and Ava, with brilliant smiles, lifted their glasses at Jack who nodded in return. He now sat alone at the bar. The leech of a girlfriend was probably in the ladies' room reapplying another layer of red permanent marker to her plumped-up lips. It wasn't like Lauren to be so bitchy, but Jack was making her crazy.

Picking up the cocktail, Lauren took a long, deep swallow, wishing she had never opened the door to a Mr. Pretty. They were too much trouble.

Chapter 5

Jack left his house early on Thursday morning with the intention of going to work. He had a ten o'clock meeting with a representative from Nike he needed to prepare for. But instead of heading to work, he found himself driving through heavy morning traffic toward Everything Nice with a blonde beauty on his mind.

It had been two days since he'd last seen Lauren at Jovi's, and thoughts of her had frequently occupied his mind ever since. And if he was completely honest with himself, since meeting her on New Year's Eve she'd made an appearance in some hot fantasies.

Normally the woman he wanted would be in his bed by now and not in his fantasies. But there was something about Lauren cautioning him to take it easy or he'd scare her away. He'd never had to work hard to get a woman. Then a thought briefly crossed his mind. He was getting older...maybe he was losing his touch? Nah, he dismissed the thought with a chuckle. So what if Lauren was proving to be more of a challenge? A little hard work never scared him. Soon he'd put the fantasy of Lauren out of his mind and into action.

He chose not to believe he wasn't Lauren's type like his mother suggested. Lauren may have tried to appear stand-offish and uninterested, but he knew women, and she gave off signals of one who was most definitely attracted. At Jovi's, when he'd touched her with a soft brush of his fingers, her body had heated up like an inferno.

Whatever the reason for the cold shoulder, Jack knew there was a hot-blooded woman sizzling beneath that cool exterior. And for the first time in a very long time, a real spark of interest ignited in his gut at the thought of melting away the ice to find the heated center.

When Jack pulled into a small carpark behind Everything Nice, next to a blue Corolla, a very sexy butt wrapped in tight, black pants poked out from the boot of the car. He couldn't see Lauren's face, but he would recognize those long legs and that ass anywhere. He'd gotten a good look at them the day they met.

For a moment, he sat in his vehicle, admiring the view of her wiggling ass. His hands twitched to touch the round sweetness, but he had the good sense to slide them into the pockets of his jeans when he got out of the car.

She appeared to be struggling with something inside the car, dropping a string of awesome curse words.

"I hope you're not hiding a body in there," he said.

Lauren jumped, smacking her head on the lid of the boot. "Shit."

Rubbing her head, she turned to face him with a fierce scowl. When she saw him her eyes widened for a beat, and then the frown deepened. But for a second he could've sworn she looked happy that he was there.

Nodding toward a heavy-looking box, he said, "I can help you with that."

A puzzled expression crossed her face, like she didn't know what he was talking about.

"The box in your car, I can get it out for you."

"No need, I can do it." She flicked a glance at the opened boot.

Dropping her hand from her head, she went back to trying to get the box out, and that ass fascinated him again. He could have stood there watching it all day. But he was raised with manners, and therefore, couldn't let her struggle with the heavy item.

"Let me help." He placed a hand on her shoulder, and she once again jumped and bumped her head.

"Shit, Jack. Stop creeping up on me!"

"Sorry, I didn't think I was. You knew I was standing right next to you." Her scowl turned fierce.

Jack bit back laughter. Even pissed off she looked sexy as hell. "So you don't think I'm creeping up on you, I'm going to reach into your car and pull out the box."

Hands on hips, she huffed. "I said I can do it."

"As much as I enjoyed the view of your wiggling ass bent over your car," he said, and she sucked in a shuddery breath, "I can't stand by and watch you pick up a heavy box."

Not waiting for her to object, he leaned in and

pulled it out. Did she mumble something about *over-processed muscles*? He wasn't winning her over like he'd planned.

"Where would you like me to put it?"

"My office is through there." Lauren pointed to a navy blue door.

Slamming the boot lid shut, she turned toward the office. The sound of a loud rip had them both looking back at the car. The flowing pink shirt she wore had gotten caught in the boot. A huge tear split the seam of her top and it gapped open, giving him a peek of her slender body and a flash of a lacy, pale pink bra.

"Dammit!" She scrambled to hold the sides of the ruined shirt together, her face turning as pink as her top. "This is all your fault." She pointed a finger at Jack with her free hand.

"My fault?"

"Yes. If you'd let me pull out the box myself, I wouldn't have ruined one of my favorite tops. But *no*, you had to turn up with your big, bulging muscles and take over."

He shook his head. "I was just trying to help. Sorry that my 'big, bulging muscles' ruined your shirt." He bit the inside of his cheek to stop from laughing.

When she propped her hands on her hips it caused the jagged edges of the shirt to fall open, giving Jack a nice view of her sexy underwear and the curve of a sweet breast. At the sight, he got an instant hard-on.

Noticing where his attention had gone, she squealed and pulled the fabric back together.

"I hope you got a good look." Sarcasm dripped like melted ice from her lips.

"A gentleman never tells."

She scoffed. "I don't see a gentleman here, only a big pervert."

This time he did laugh, then he put the box down at her feet and headed back to his car.

"Where are you going? You're not going to leave me here like this, are you?" she called after him and shot a nervous glance around the empty carpark.

Oh, now she wants help. He chuckled to himself as he opened the back passenger door, unzipped his gym bag, and pulled out a Flaming Stars t-shirt. Walking back, he held it out to Lauren.

She narrowed her eyes. "Is it clean?"

"I ran for an hour in it and then pumped some weights. It stinks a bit, but what other options do you have?" When she screwed up her nose he said, "Of course it's clean."

She snatched it from his outstretched hand, turned her back to him, and slid it over the damaged top. The baggy t-shirt fell below her butt. Images of her wearing nothing but it while he ran his hands up her smooth, creamy legs had his stomach tied in knots. His hands itched to touch her, and it needed to be soon.

"Thanks for the shirt. After I get this box inside I'll go home and change. I can drop it off at your office if you like." Turning back toward him, the anger she had thrown at him a moment ago had dissipated. She ducked her head and averted her gaze.

"Keep it. I have dozens of them."

A tentative smile tugged at her lips. "So, do you think your big, bulging muscles can bring the box into my office?"

Jack linked his fingers together and stretched his arms in front of him before picking up the box. "I'll give it a go."

This time she laughed, and the husky, sexy sound sent a surge of heat to his throbbing crotch. It was a good thing he held the box in front of him.

Jack followed Lauren into a small office—a room leading off the shop—and placed the box on the floor next to the desk then took a moment to glance around the tidy room. She'd decorated the space with dainty knick-knacks and soft furnishings. Photos of Lauren smiling and laughing with the two women he'd met at Jovi's lined the walls. Her office was too feminine for his taste, but it had been decorated with style and sophistication.

"Why are you here, Jack?"

Why was he there? He wanted her naked and in his bed. But he didn't think she'd want to hear what was really on his mind, so instead he said, "I'd like to take you out to dinner."

Her eyes widened, then she slowly shook her head. "Sorry, I'm busy."

"I haven't told you when."

"When were you thinking?"

"Tonight."

"I'm busy." She tidied up a stack of papers on the desk.

"Tomorrow night?"

Brushing her fingers through the ends of her hair, she said, "Busy tomorrow too."

He crossed his arms over his chest. "You're not going to tell me you're washing your hair, are you?"

Guilt spread across her face. "Of course I'm not."

He didn't believe her for a second. "Then you tell me when you're available."

"I'm not available." She rearranged a bunch of red and yellow folders sitting in an already tidy tray.

"Are you involved with someone?" Did his mother get the information wrong?

"No, I'm not."

So what was the problem? Because he didn't believe the crap about being too goodlooking. "What about a drink then if you don't have time for dinner?"

Sighing, she sat on the edge of the desk. "Look, Jack, I'm not interested in going to dinner or for a drink." Then, like she thought she should soften the rejection, she added, "But thanks for asking."

Jack wasn't one to back down from a challenge. He'd led his team to victory more times than he could count when no one gave them a chance. Giving up wasn't an option.

As he walked toward the desk, wary eyes trailed him with a mix of trepidation and suspicion. He stood close enough for his leg to brush against her hip, and satisfaction at the sound of her quick, shuddery breath pulled a smile from his lips.

Leaning closer, he breathed in the sweet fragrance of her perfume. "Meet me tonight."

The pulse in her neck beat at a rapid pace, and he desperately wanted to run his tongue along it. Wanted to taste the sweat running off her body when he got her into bed.

She slid along the desk and pushed herself away. "No, Jack."

"I'll be at Jovi's if you change your mind."

"I won't. If you want to buy another gift, Jaime will be more than happy to help you, otherwise, we're done here." She marched to the door leading to the carpark and opened it.

For now he'd let it go. With a brief nod, he left her office. Once sitting in the car, his lips curled up into a smile. Yes, she was a challenge he was eagerly up for.

Chapter 6

Hazel eyes with golden flecks of arousal stared up at him. Her tongue darted out and licked her plump bottom lip in anticipation of his next move. Honey-blonde hair as smooth as silk fanned over the pillow as Lauren lay naked beneath him. Firm, pert breasts fit generously in his hands. Her rosy nipples stood proudly at attention. Lowering his head, Jack took the pink offering into his mouth. Lauren groaned, and it was the sexiest sound he'd ever heard. She arched her back up off the bed, sealing their damp bodies together.

"Please," she whimpered.

"What do you want?" he whispered, then blew warm air across the raised peaks.

"You. I want you. Now." A shiver passed through her body as he trailed his fingers down her soft, flushed skin and entered her hot, wet center.

"Where do you want me?" His voice shook. He might be teasing her, but it was killing him to hold back.

"Oh God, Jack. There. I want you there. Now!" The last word was said in a pleading sob.

Rising above her, he kissed her slow and deep, then positioned himself between eagerly awaiting thighs. Lauren grabbed his hips with impatient hands, digging her nails into his flesh and guiding him to where she wanted him…

The sudden shrill of his mobile phone pulled Jack out of the erotic dream. Blinking, he turned his head to the pillow next to him. When Lauren wasn't laying naked by his side, he let out a string of curses, crude enough to blister the ears of the toughest truckies.

He fumbled with the phone sitting on the bedside table, punched the *answer* button, and growled, "What?"

"I'm so sorry to disturb you, Jack, but we have a big problem at the office," Jack's receptionist Ellen stammered.

Jack glanced at the green illuminated time on the alarm clock and swore under his breath. He'd been enjoying the dream about Lauren so much he'd slept through the alarm. He should have already been on his way to the office.

"What's the problem, Ellen?" he asked.

"I came into work early this morning and…" Her voice cracked.

Hearing the distress in her voice he shot out of bed and pulled clothes from the wardrobe.

Ellen started working for him after he'd taken over Henderson's. She'd just been getting back into the workforce. One look at her and Jack had known that a woman who'd raised four boys knew a lot about organization and time management; something he desperately needed help with. She'd proved capable, and reliable, and ran his office like a drill sergeant. Nothing rattled her. Expect now. She sounded extremely upset.

"Someone has broken into the office," she finally managed to say. "It's such a mess, everything's ruined."

"Get out of there," he commanded while shoving his legs into jeans.

"I'm outside. It's terrible, Jack. I haven't called the police yet. Should I call them now?" She sniffed.

"No, wait until I get there. I'll be there in five minutes." He hung up, threw the rest of his clothes on, and ran out the door.

An explosion of papers and destroyed furniture littered Jack's office. Ellen hadn't been exaggerating when she said everything had been ruined. Standing amongst the chaos, his body quivered with anger as he looked around him.

Papers scattered the carpet like confetti and the desk lay on its side with deep crevices gouged into the shiny mahogany. Three torn football jerseys, that he'd won premierships in, lay in shreds at his feet. He clenched his hands into fists at the shattered glass scattered around them.

He'd worked damn hard and sweated his ass off wearing those jerseys.

The black, Italian-leather sofa where he sat to have his morning coffee while looking over the day's reports was now carved up like a Christmas turkey, its stuffing thrown all over the room. Chairs were stripped of their fabric and the legs had been splintered and tossed around the room. On the largest wall, directly behind where his desk should have been, in red paint dripped the word *asshole*.

The destruction and the hostile word written on the wall told him exactly who was responsible. The last time he'd seen Claire she'd been screaming at him in this very room.

There was no point calling the police. There was no solid proof, and he didn't want to

explain the sordid details to them. And if he were truly honest with himself, he *had* been an asshole. Getting involved with her had been unprofessional and never should have happened. If Claire had done the damage, which he'd bet his left nut to be true, he hoped she'd gotten the revenge out of her system.

The disaster zone needed to be cleared. He needed to organize a cleanup crew to haul everything out. He'd also need a painter and new office equipment and furniture. The more he looked around, the longer the list grew. Nothing had been spared. Claire had been one pissed off woman, and he'd underestimated her anger.

With his hands in his pockets, he walked around the room, kicking the debris out of the way. Jack heard Ellen in the reception area already organizing a company to come out. He had to remember to add a good bonus to her next paycheck.

Before taking over the business the office had previously been his father's, and his mother had decorated it. The only things Jack added were the football photos and jerseys he'd hung on the walls.

Remembering that his mother recently had a bedroom redecorated, he thought about calling and asking who she'd hired. But his parents had left for a holiday in Perth two days ago, and he didn't want to worry them.

Jack pulled his phone from the pocket of his jeans and dialed Leah's number, hoping she could help.

"Hey you," she answered on a flustered breath.

He could hear his niece crying in the background, so he got straight to the point. "Hi, Leah, can you tell me the name of the woman who did some decorating for Mum? I think she may have decorated her bedroom."

"Why? Are you planning on hanging flowery curtains in your room with matching pink, fluffy pillows for your bed?" She laughed.

"Very funny. Who was it?"

"The woman works at the place where you bought Mum's mirror. I think her name is Laura or something like that."

"Lauren," he corrected.

The image of sultry hazel eyes and creamy skin entered his mind. His balls tightened as he remembered the dream he'd been rudely woken from. Frenzied hands had gripped his hips, waiting for him to take the plunge. He would've loved to have finished the dream. God, he would love to taste the real thing, but he couldn't think of that right now while on the phone with his sister.

"Why do you need a decorator?"

"I'll explain later. I've got to go." He hung up.

He left the messy office, telling Ellen he had a few things he needed to take care of and to keep the doors locked until the cleaning crew arrived. She assured him she'd be fine and to take all the time he needed.

Heat surrounded him as he left the office, and he could feel it seeping through his black tshirt. The sun bounced off parked cars and the glass of shopfront windows. The early January morning already promised to be a scorcher. He walked the short distance to his car, slid onto the warm leather seats, and drove with anticipation to Lauren's shop.

Chapter 7

"*E*arth to Lauren!" A hand waved in front of Lauren's face, making her jump in surprise.

She'd been miles away, staring at a blank computer screen.

The smudge of freckles on Jaime's nose crinkled as she laughed. Jaime had started working for Lauren two years ago after finishing high school, looking for a part-time job to help pay her way through university. Upon getting to know Jaime, Lauren discovered that their stories weren't dissimilar. Jaime had also come from a home which offered no support or much love and affection. And even though Jaime didn't have good role models in her life she'd come out of the turbulent environment as a caring and respectful young woman. Lauren felt a bond toward Jaime, and made a promise to herself that she would help Jaime out whenever she needed it.

"Your spreadsheets can't be that engrossing." She

poked her head around to see what Lauren was looking at but frowned when she noticed the blank screen.

Lauren blamed her distraction on the late night with the girls, drinking too many cocktails Ava had made. She was getting too old for excessive drinking. Those days had passed. But Jade had needed cheering up. Her cousin Caitlyn had broken up with her fiancé and Jade swore it was because of the Brennan curse and she was doomed to live a lonely life.

Lauren needed to blame the distraction on the alcohol because she didn't want to admit that the lapse of concentration was due to a sexy sports star in tight jeans and a drop-dead, gorgeous face. She hadn't told Ava and Jade about Jack's visit and the invitation to dinner. After the song and dance they'd made about their first meeting she didn't need them performing a whole Broadway show.

Now Jaime was standing in front of her with a bemused look. Her long, dark brown hair tied up in a high ponytail swung behind her head. Her smooth, creamy skin was absent of makeup apart from a swipe of cherry red lip-gloss, and she wore a soft yellow maxi dress with tiny, white flowers. How long had Lauren stared vaguely at the computer before Jaime finally got her attention? She didn't need her to ask questions about why she was so absent-minded.

Shuffling some papers around to appear as if she'd gone back to work, she said, "I'm sorry, Jaime. What's up?"

"I've got some packages to take to the post office before customers start coming in. Do you have time to come out to the front or would you like me to wait?"

"No, you can go now. I'll be out in a minute."

Waving, Jaime left the office, and Lauren heard the tinkering bells of the front door as she left. Before Lauren had time to get out of the chair, the bells tinkered again.

"Jaime must have forgotten something," she mumbled. But when Jaime didn't call out or come back into the office she assumed there was a customer waiting. She rose, straightened her skirt, and entered the shop.

As if she'd plucked him out of her daydreams, Jack stood in front of a display of crystal vases, looking a million times better than any dream ever could. When she entered the shop Jack turned and flashed an oh-so-sexy smile. Her stomach did a funny flip-flop and she could hear her heart pounding.

She was in a whole lot of trouble if one smile made her insides turn to mush.

Watching Lauren standing in the threshold of the shop, he could have sworn, for a moment, a flash of pleasure lit up her eyes at seeing him. But just as quickly as it had appeared, it disappeared. Today she wore her hair tied back. His fingers itched to run through it, tousle it up, and give it back its bedroom look of his dream.

"Hi, Jack." Her voice sounded husky and incredibly sexy.

She cleared her throat and fiddled with the silver

locket, drawing his gaze down to her cleavage exposed by the V-neck, coral-colored top. Noticing where his gaze had drifted to, she snatched her hand away.

"I'm assuming you're in need of a gift?" With hand on her hip, a firm, frosty tone replaced her husky, sexy voice. Like she had remembered she didn't want to be around him for some reason. He'd really like to know why.

What had he done to cause the ice in the air? A dinner invitation surely couldn't result in such a cold shoulder.

"No, I don't need a gift."

She raised her palms in the air then dropped them by her sides. "Then what do you want?"

Never before had he needed to charm a woman into going out with him. But she was proving to not easily be swayed.

He wasn't foolish enough to believe that the women he *associated* with wanted him for his great company. Fame and fortune attracted them. They made no secret about it, and as long as they understood the relationship would never be a long-lasting one, he was okay with that.

Most relationships didn't last in the professional football world. It was a demanding sport. Training, games, traveling, and social events took up a huge amount of their time. Groupies were always a temptation, and sometimes too much for any man to refuse. It was a hard life for wives and girlfriends, and most couldn't handle it. He'd once experienced the strain his career put on a relationship, and didn't want to put anyone else through that again.

But Lauren didn't seem to give two shits about his fame. In fact, he sensed it was more of a turnoff.

When he'd introduced himself on New Year's Eve, and recognition dawned on her, the temperature in the room had immediately dropped ten degrees, when earlier heat had been simmering. Lauren may have wanted to hide it, but he knew better. She was cool and uninterested on the outside but as hot as a firecracker on the inside.

Trailing a lazy gaze from her head to her toes, he answered, "I want you."

Lauren's face flushed bright red. "I told you yesterday I'm not interested."

"I haven't explained what I want." Images of her exposed creamy white breasts wrapped in flimsy pink lace had him wanting to explore the rest of her. That was what he really wanted, but for now he'd keep that information to himself.

"I don't want to hear it." She touched the silver locket again.

"How do you know you don't want to hear what I have to say? You might like it." He grinned.

Lauren dropped her hands from the locket, placed them on her hips, and narrowed her eyes. "Forget it, Jack. I'm not interested. How dare you come back in here and proposition me after I already told you I'm not interested? Didn't you get the message loud and clear yesterday? And throwing me those sexy eyes isn't going to make me change my mind. Did you expect me to fall at your feet because you told me *you want me*? So no, Jack, my answer is no," she said as her chest puffed in and out.

Digging his hands into his pockets, Jack rocked back on his heels. The misunderstanding amused him, but he had to admit he wasn't completely innocent in her confusion. He tried keeping a straight face, but the corners of his lips twitched. "If you had let me explain before jumping down my throat, I would have told you I want you for a job."

Confusion creased her brow. "A job?"

"Someone broke into my office and trashed it last night. Every piece of furniture is ruined, pictures on the walls…everything. I want to hire you to redecorate it for me."

He watched a display of varying shades of red travel across her face and felt a small tug of guilt for embarrassing her. But part of him thought she had it coming. Maybe she'd eventually heat up and melt away the ice queen.

"You… I thought… Sexy eyes…" she stuttered.

"I'm sorry I didn't make myself clear." Not really, but he didn't think it was a good idea to mention it.

But she must have seen by his expression that he was far from sorry. Her eyes hardened and golden flecks shot through them. She slowly sauntered closer and stood directly in front of him. The high heels she wore not only made her long legs look amazing but brought their faces level, and she jabbed a finger in his chest.

"How could you let me rave on like that?" *Jab.* "You could have stopped me from making a complete idiot of myself." *Jab.* "You deliberately tricked me with your smooth voice and lusty eyes." *Jab. Jab.* "And you enjoyed every minute of it." *Jab. Jab. Jab.* "I don't want your stinking job. I want you out of my shop now!" *Jab.*

Jack's shoulders shook with laughter, which only made her look even angrier. "I'll pay you whatever you want."

"I don't want your money." *Jab.* "You can stick your money up your—"

Jack caught the poking finger and held it in a firm grip. She struggled to free herself, but he held tight. "You didn't exactly misunderstand me. Trust me when I tell you I do *want* you." Drawing in an unsteady breath, her gaze dropped to his mouth. *Yeah, there's that heat.*

He leaned closer until their faces were only inches apart. The sweet smell of flowers and sunshine tormented him, making him want to explore and touch every part of her. "I want you, Lauren, and I know you're feeling something too."

This time he let her snatch her hand away, and she stomped behind the counter. "I don't want the job. Find someone else." She avoided discussing the attraction between them. He'd let it go for now.

"I'm a desperate man. What can I do to change your mind?"

"I won't change my mind. Now, if you'll excuse me, I have a lot of work to do." She turned her attention to a box of trinkets on the counter. He'd been dismissed.

Jack pulled his wallet from his back pocket and slid a business card along the smooth counter. "Here's my card. If you change your mind, call me."

Leaving her shop, he shook his head. Dammit, she'd rejected him *again.*

Chapter 8

"**A**rrggh!" Groaning, Lauren flicked the lock and hung the *back in five minutes* sign.

God, she needed a few minutes to pull herself together. Storming into the office, she flung herself down on the chair, and threw Jack's business card into the bin next to the desk.

Jack had made her look like a complete fool. Letting her believe he wanted her for hot and sexy kind of stuff. Well, he actually did, but he should have made it clear from the start that he had a job offer. If he had, then the whole embarrassing moment could've been avoided.

He wanted her, but she would not be another woman added to his long list of conquests. No, she wasn't stupid enough to fall for the smooth-talking, good-looking football hero. She'd fallen for a pretty face and smooth-talker before, and it only caused her terrible heartache. Safer to stay far, far away and never think of him again.

There was too much work to do and she couldn't stay

in the office brooding over one annoying, yet sexy as hell, man. With the decision made, she went back into the store and planned to wipe him from her mind.

But as the day went on Lauren learned it was impossible to not think about Jack. She'd rung up the wrong amount in sales, dropped and smashed a crystal champagne flute, and knocked over a display of greeting cards all because images of green eyes and a sexy smile kept invading her thoughts. She needed to get Jack out of her head before the shop got destroyed.

Lauren could tell Jaime wondered what the hell was wrong. She'd asked Lauren if she was feeling sick and needed to lie down. Yeah, she had a sickness all right, and its name was Jack Henderson. He was infecting her mind and body like a bad disease—heating her skin and blazing through every molecule of her body. The cure? She didn't think there was one other than distance, and that's what she planned on doing. There was no reason they needed to spend any time together, so it shouldn't take too long for the memory of Jack to fade.

Around four-thirty the shop slowed down, so Jaime went home early. Because she couldn't afford any more breakages, Lauren also called it a day.

Going through the store, switching off lights, she made her way back to the office to check her emails. A bunch filled her inbox and she sorted through them, then sent one to a manufacturer regarding the bracelet order she'd placed two weeks ago before shutting down the computer. When she picked up her phone and keys from the desk, the phone vibrated in her hand. Not recognizing the number, she swiped the screen to answer the call.

"Hello." She hoped it would be a quick conversation. She wanted to go home, pour a glass of wine, and forget about her day.

"Hey, sis. Long time, no hear."

Icy dread slithered like a snake over her skin. With dread Lauren dropped back down on the chair.

Wandering around the office, Jack took in the empty room, and his body tensed at the sight. For Claire to go to such great measures he must have really pissed her off. He'd known having sex with her was a bad idea, but how was he to know that she'd go all *fatal attraction* on him? There better not be a dead bunny cooking in a pot when he got home. Well, if she wanted to pay him back for rejecting her, job well done.

There wasn't anything he could do there until morning, so he locked up and walked the short distance to his car, which he'd parked out on the street instead of the underground carpark.

It would've made life easier if Lauren had taken the job. What did he know about decorating and all that crap? A desk to hold a computer and a chair to sit on was good enough for him, but he knew he needed to do more than that. Could he wait three weeks until his mother returned from holidays and ask for help? Not unless he wanted to sit on the floor for the next few weeks. He needed someone now. He would've asked Leah to help, but she was busy with the new baby he didn't want to trouble her.

Coming up with a way to change Lauren's mind could be difficult. Whatever bug she had up her ass had stopped her from taking the job. Maybe what his mother said about her not associating with anyone like him wasn't totally bullshit after all.

As he reached his black BMW he noticed it was tilted at an odd angle. "Great. A flat tire."

Crouching down to take a closer look, he saw not one but two flat tires. Rubbing a hand along the warm rubber, he discovered they'd been slashed.

Pushing himself up, he stormed around the other side of the car. What he found on the driver's side was a long, white stripe etched deep into the sleek, black paint.

"Fuck!" he said, kicking the tire and pushing fingers through his hair.

Fury trembled in his chest like a rumbling train. The bitch had gone too far; she'd fucked with his car. His office was one thing, but to trash his car…

You didn't mess with a man's wheels and expect to get away with it. He needed to shut her down.

After calling a taxi to drive him home to pick up his Landcruiser, Jack stood on Claire's veranda, banging on the front door. Peeling paint cracked and fell to the ground from the force of his blows. Clenching his fist as he waited for her to open the door, fury boiled in his gut like a bubbling volcano. He took a few deep breaths to calm down. Nope, it didn't work.

Never in his life had he felt so much anger toward a woman. Needing to take the aggravation out on something, he pounded on the door again. This time the blows were so hard he was surprised his hand didn't break through the flimsy timber.

The whole office-trashing was easy to let pass. Yes, it was a big, expensive mess, but it had been his fault for leading her on. But she had gone way too far with his car. He still didn't want to bring the police into it, but he sure as hell would deal with her.

A sharp voice stopped him from breaking the door down. "Would you stop bangin' on that flamin' door?"

Turning, he saw a man in his early to mid-sixties approach him. He was dressed in worn, navy work shorts and a faded yellow t-shirt with the words *that's life* peeling off the fabric. Gray, wispy hair peeked out from underneath a worn green and red cap. He walked with a slight limp, stopping to lean his forearms on the timber railing. A cigarette dangled precariously from his cracked lips.

"Sorry, I didn't mean to disturb you, but I'm looking for Claire. Do you know when she'll be home?"

The older man squinted through the fading light and trail of smoke, his gaze assessing

Jack. He was used to people staring at him, trying to figure out where they'd seen him before.

When recognition hit, the old man's eyebrows disappeared inside his cap. "You're Jack Henderson!" he stated happily.

Jack smiled—the polite smile reserved for times like this. "Yes, I am."

"I was sorry to see you retire so early. You were great for the team."

"Thank you."

The man took the cigarette from his mouth and spat a gob of spit into the weed-infested garden. "They should never have let Stevens and Coleman on the team. Don't know what the coaches were thinking letting them play. They can't pass a ball for shit. The Stars were lucky they didn't lose the premiership last season."

Jack agreed. He didn't know what the coaches and management had been thinking either, but he didn't have time to get into it. This man seemed like the type who could stand around all day talking about footy. Normally Jack didn't mind, he loved the game and understood people's passion, but he had more important things to do. He needed to find Claire.

Pointing to the front door before the man brought up more footy talk, Jack asked, "Do you know the woman who lives here?"

"She's my next-door neighbor," he answered.

"Do you have any idea what time she gets home?"

Claire's neighbor scratched the side of his head. "My missus said she saw her leaving this morning with a carload of luggage. Claire told her she was going on a holiday and would be gone a while. My missus didn't believe her. She reckons she had to take off because she wasn't paying the rent." He lifted his cap and ran his hand through his hair. "I'll miss having her around. She was real good to look at." He laughed and slapped the cap he was holding on the side of his leg.

Jack let out a frustrated breath and handed him a business card. "Call me if she happens to come back."

The man's eyes lit up like he'd given him a winning lottery ticket.

"Sure thing, Jack."

"Thanks for your help." Jack waved goodbye and jogged down the cracked veranda steps before the old man could start talking about footy again.

With angry strides he reached the car, swung open the Landcruiser's door with force, then climbed in the driver's seat and pulled out on the street. Jack hoped his car would be ready in a couple of days. He had paid extra to have it done as quickly as possible. God help the bitch if she laid one dirty finger on it again.

Chapter 9

"What do you want, Belinda?" Lauren shivered as if a freezing July wind blew through her body. *The same as always*, she thought —*money*. Over the years Belinda had attached herself to Lauren like a leech and was sucking her dry.

"I thought my lil' sis would be excited to hear from me since it's been so long." Sarcasm packed like a punch in Belinda's voice.

"How much do you need this time?" Lauren's relationship with Belinda had always been hostile. She didn't remember a single time when they laughed and had fun like sisters usually did. Never had they played with dolls, done each other's hair, or told each other their deepest secrets.

With a harsh snigger through the phone, Belinda said, "I don't know why you're still keeping your dirty little secret? But I'm not goin' to complain."

No, Belinda wouldn't complain, because Lauren was

her own personal cash cow. All she had to do was wave Graham in front of her face and Lauren handed over the money. Belinda believed Lauren didn't want the affair made public because she was protecting him. In her sick, twisted mind she thought Lauren still idolized Graham because of his power and money. If she knew Lauren was only trying to protect herself, she'd run to the media with the story about the affair just to make Lauren's life absolutely miserable.

Graham now covered major events around the globe and had become one of the highest paid journalists, not only in Australia, but also around the world.

If the media ever found out about the affair, Lauren's life and privacy would become a circus. She didn't need her painful past plastered all over the evening news. She'd worked too damn hard to get her life on track for the tabloids to rip it apart.

After telling Belinda about the baby, Lauren had let the name of the father slip out. She'd felt the need to defend herself because Belinda was accusing her of spreading her legs for anyone desperate enough to have her and she claimed Lauren wouldn't know who the father was. There was no way she could convince Belinda that Graham had been the only man she'd ever slept with. Belinda laughed and didn't believe it, saying someone like him wouldn't touch her with a ten-foot pole.

Lauren immediately regretted blurting it out and told Belinda she'd made it up just so she'd drop it. It was then Belinda knew Lauren was telling the truth. They both knew Lauren was a bad liar.

Belinda talked about selling the spicy details to a magazine. Not that she knew them, but she could make something up and they'd pay a fortune for them.

The only way to get Belinda to keep quiet about the affair was to give her all the jewelry Graham had showered her with. That had been the easy part; Lauren couldn't bear to look at them let alone put any of that cold metal and diamonds next to her skin. They'd only serve as a reminder of everything Graham had pretended to be. Belinda, on the other hand, had hit the jackpot.

Lauren met Graham during a night out at Dicey's Pub after spilling a drink on him. Once recovered from the embarrassment and being star-struck, they ended up talking for hours. Later, back at the hotel he was staying at, they fell into bed with more urgent things to do than talk.

The next few weeks had been the greatest whirlwind of Lauren's life. They continued to meet in luxurious hotels to make love like crazy. Then, to show how much he loved her, even though he never said the words, Graham would shower Lauren with expensive jewelry. Lauren had fallen madly in love.

Lauren entered the lift in the lobby of the Four Seasons and punched the number of the floor where Graham had a room. Glimpsing her reflection in the mirrors lining the wall, she caressed her stomach gently and smiled a secret smile.

The last few mornings she'd woken up feeling sick, and

when she missed her period, she decided to do a home pregnancy test. When two bright pink lines showed a positive result, shock slammed into her. How could she be pregnant? Graham always used a condom. Well, except for that one time in the shower, and as a result, she was going to have his baby.

Shock soon turned to excitement because she'd found the man of her dreams and they would have a happy family. And she couldn't wait to tell him the wonderful news.

When she arrived at the harbor view suite, Graham was already waiting for her. Normally, she would have taken the time to appreciate the breathtaking view of Sydney Harbor and the Sydney Opera House, but she was too excited to do any of that.

As always, Graham had champagne and strawberries waiting, not that she'd drink the champagne now that she had a precious life to take care of. Also, a blue Tiffany & Company box sat next to the crystal flute, another gift to show her how much he cared.

Rushing over, she threw her arms around his neck. Graham greeted her with a long, passionate kiss, and tugged the zipper down on the back of her dress. He was in a hurry. He must need to get to work.

His work demanded a lot of his time, so on days when he had to rush off they made love fast. But before she lost herself in the drugging kiss, she pulled free to tell him the exciting news.

Impatience showed on his face and strong hands grabbed her around the waist, smashing their bodies together. Giggling, she placed her hands on his heaving chest and pushed away from his alluring mouth. "Stop. I have wonderful news to tell you."

"It can wait. I can't. Take off your clothes," he said, loosening his tie and hanging it on the back of a chair. He reached for her again, but she quickly stepped away.

"It can't wait. I'm so excited I want to tell you now, and then we can celebrate however you like." She slid her hand up his chest, trying to sound seductive, wanting to be more sophisticated for him, but she never could pull it off.

"Hurry up then. I don't have much time," he said as he unbuttoned his shirt.

Sighing over being hurried, she said, "I hate when you have to rush off. I was hoping we'd spend the night together."

"I can't, I have to be up early for work in the morning," he snapped.

When her eyes widen at his tone, he placed soothing hands on either side of her face and kissed her gently on the lips. "I'm sorry, darling. I didn't mean to snap at you. I'm busy, that's all. What is it you have to tell me?"

Taking a shaky breath, nerves suddenly crept in about telling him about the baby. But she let the words spill out before she lost the nerve. "I'm pregnant."

Color drained from his face, and he stepped away. "What?"

The quietly spoken word had the effect of an icy blast. Lauren rubbed her arms to ward off the chill, her excitement from moments ago slipping away along with her smile.

Red replaced his colorless complexion, and his eyes grew as dark as the devil's. "You slut!"

"W-what?" Lauren stammered as she stumbled back from the explosion of his fury.

"How many guys have you fucked while you've been with me? And now you think you can claim that the bastard is mine?" He laughed without mirth. "I know what you're trying to do."

Shock at his reaction left her speechless.

A finger as deadly as a pistol pointed in her face. "You're after my money."

Because the words caught behind the lump in her throat, she shook her head rapidly.

He gave her a cruel scoff. "Don't think I don't know about the shithole you live in. I'm your ticket out of that slum."

Finally finding her voice, as weak and shaky as it was, she managed to say, "The baby's yours. I haven't been with anyone else. I don't want your money. I love you, and I thought you loved me too." Hot tears poured down her face.

For a second Graham froze, then he threw back his head and laughed hard and harsh.

He picked up his suit jacket lying on the bed and then his tie and draped them over his arm.

"You stupid little girl. You were a good fuck, that was all."

The cruel comment was like a slap to the face, and she drew in a sharp breath. Her legs couldn't hold her up any longer, and she stumbled to the nearest chair.

Pulling his wallet out from the jacket's pocket, he thumbed through one hundred dollar notes and threw them on the bed. "This should be enough to get rid of the bastard."

As if protecting the baby from the ugliness of his words, she splayed her trembling hands over her stomach.

"If you dare go to the media about this, I will make your life a living hell. Do you understand?"

The green notes were scattered across the bed and she stared at them numbly.

"Do you understand?" he shouted.

Jumping, she then nodded weakly.

When Graham spun on his heels and stormed toward the door, she didn't watch him leave; her eyes were too full of tears and broken dreams.

Three months later, Lauren experienced another shock. She had just come back from her doctor's appointment, excitement bubbling because she heard the baby's heartbeat for the first time. The wonders of having a little human growing inside her filled her with such awe she could hardly stop smiling.

After the appointment, she'd planned to meet Jade at a coffee shop not far from campus.

While waiting for Jade's class to finish she picked up a copy of New Idea, a magazine she'd never admit she enjoyed reading, and flicked through the glossy pages. Her hand stilled on the third page, and the blood in her veins turned to ice.

Beaming up at her from the glossy page was Graham's handsome face. Sitting next to him was a beautiful woman with emerald green eyes and gorgeous, long, black hair placed neatly over her shoulder. A tiny sleeping baby bundled in a soft pink wrap lay nestled in her arms. The headline read: Graham's Little Miracle Melts his Heart of Stone.

The magazine trembled in her hands and it fell to the ground. Lauren was pregnant with a married man's baby!

"Are you listening to me?" Belinda's agitated voice droned down the phone line, bringing Lauren back to the present.

"No, I wasn't," she answered honestly.

She heard Belinda's scoff. "You always did think you were so much better than me."

Merely being a decent person made Lauren better than Belinda, but she'd keep that thought to herself. "What do you want?"

She should have asked *how much do you want?* The sooner Belinda named her price, the sooner this unpleasant phone call could end. "If you'd been listenin' you'd know."

"Tell me again," Lauren said.

She did a quick calculation of how much money she had in the bank and how much she could spare. It probably wouldn't leave her with very much, but she'd just have to cut back on her spending for a few weeks. She really didn't need to eat, right? It would be worth starving if it meant getting Belinda out of her life for a few more months.

"Mum's had a stroke. The ol' bitch is in the hospital."

"What?"

"Got your attention now, have I?" Belinda laughed harshly.

Yes, Belinda had her attention, and Lauren tried to process how she felt about the news.

A moment later she came to the conclusion she felt no sadness or despair whatsoever.

Should she visit her in the hospital? No, she'd cut all ties with her mother years ago.

Dorothy had never been a mother to her. She'd never given her a moment of her time and attention. Years of neglect and lack of affection wiped out any feelings Lauren had for her. The grief Lauren should have over the loss, or near loss, of a parent did not exist.

Lauren may not have a relationship with their mother, but Belinda did. Even though they constantly fought with each other Belinda and their mother were always a unit, no matter how unconventional it was. So hearing Belinda sound so unfeeling about their mother's health showed Lauren yet again how heartless her sister could be.

"If you'd been listenin' I was trying to explain to you that Mum had a stroke two days ago. They expect me to pay for all this extra stuff, like special care and a bunch of other crap," she complained. "We both know I don't have the money."

Two days. Belinda waited two days to tell her their mother was in the hospital? And probably only mentioned it because she needed the money to pay the expenses.

She asked Belinda how much she'd need. Belinda gave her an exorbitant amount.

"You can't be serious?" She almost fell off the chair.

She had a gut feeling not all the money was going toward bills.

"These things are expensive."

"I don't have that much." Lauren thought again about the money in her account. She had worried she wouldn't eat for a few weeks, but with the amount Belinda was asking for she wouldn't be able to eat for a year.

"Well, *I* don't have it. I'm broke," Belinda snapped.

Maybe if Belinda stopped spending money on alcohol and who knew what else she'd have some saved. But why bother saving when she could call Lauren and demand more?

"Why do I have to pay for it all?" she asked, trying hard to stay calm.

"All the years of stress and trouble you caused was what triggered the stroke."

Lauren laughed harshly. She couldn't believe Belinda's accusation. She'd always tried to be the perfect daughter, because then, maybe, her mother would love her. But nothing she did was ever good enough.

"It couldn't have been all the booze and smokes she loved so much that brought on the stroke?" she asked sarcastically.

"You're such a bitch, Lauren. You can never do anything wrong. I need the money,"

Belinda spat. "*You* better pay."

Lauren rubbed her fingers wearily against her temple. "I told you I don't have that much." Then her eyes flicked down to the business card in the bin. She wished she had a better way of getting the money, but her options were slim to none.

"I can always ask Graham for it. I'm sure his lovely wife would be very interested to hear all about your secret love affair."

So many times Lauren had been tempted to let Belinda tell the world about the affair. She'd wanted everyone to know what a dirty, cheating snake Graham was. He deserved to lose everything he held dear, just like she had. If only she didn't care what the outcome would do to her.

If Belinda had gone to the media, she would've been paid a generous amount of money for the story. But it would have been a one-off payment. This way, she had Lauren as her personal ATM and access to money whenever she wanted it.

"Do I ask Mr. and Mrs. Stone for the money?" Belinda asked with mocking sweetness.

Lauren glanced back down at Jack's card. He told her he was prepared to pay whatever she wanted to redecorate his office. It felt like a fist squeezed tight around her chest, and she took a deep breath. She knew what needed to be done.

"I'll give you the money," Lauren said, picking the card out of the bin. "But I'm going to need about a month to get it to you."

"I want it now," Belinda snapped, sounding desperate for it. Again Lauren wondered how much really was for medical bills and how much was for Belinda.

"I told you I don't have it, but I can get it. The end of

the month is the best I can do. I'll call you when I have it and arrange a time to drop it off to you. Unless you'd rather I deposit it into your account?"

"I want cash."

She figured as much.

"I'll see you in a month." Lauren hung up.

Chapter 10

"How dare he fucking do this to me!" Claire flung her bulky luggage onto the cheap, threadbare bedspread covering a squeaky mattress. The bed, with an old, scratched faux timber headboard, dominated the small room. The hotel room she rented had free Foxtel that viewed adult-only channels, and it smelled of stale smoke and sex.

Why did she think Jack was different? Because he was kind and looked at her with love.

But when he'd gotten what he wanted he'd dumped her like rotten garbage.

Pacing the small, cramped room, she ran her hands through her tangled hair, tugging hard at the roots. "Arghh!" she screamed at the peeling wallpaper. "You promised to love me. You said you'd take me away from this life!" She wildly swung her arms around, taking in the cheap room.

Screaming again, she pounded her fists against her temples.

She'd gone back to his office on Thursday, hoping Jack would see what a huge mistake letting her go was, but the office was empty. Breaking in, with the intention of waiting for him, a red haze of rage consumed her and she ended up destroying the office. The desk he'd screwed her on had been the initial target, but before she knew it, she started tearing through the rest of the room.

The adrenaline rush kept her pumped for hours. Even daring to sit across the road at Mandy's Coffee House the next morning, sipping iced tea while she watched the comings and goings from the office. Ellen had been so scared. Not that she had anything against her, but it made Claire giggle when she watched Ellen run out of the office looking like she'd seen a ghost.

It hadn't taken long for Jack to arrive. Bursting out of his car, he said a few words to Ellen, and then entered the office. His hair was rumpled and he sported morning stubble. His wrinkled jeans and t-shirt looked like he'd picked them up from the bedroom floor. To say he looked mad as hell was an understatement. She hadn't wanted to make him mad. Had only wanted him to know he couldn't treat her like a whore. She thought she meant more to him than that. She was sure of it. He was just taking a little longer to realize it.

But as she sat and watched, a moment of anger had fueled her mind, twisting thoughts around in her head, telling her he was like every other man who'd screwed her then left. She got another chance to sink her shiny new knife into his chest. His black BMW Coupe.

Jack's pride and joy.

He left it parked at the front of the building, glistening in the morning sun, and she couldn't resist. With people constantly walking past it had been a huge risk. But she pretended to bend down to fix her shoe, all the while stamping the car with her artwork.

The screeching sound, made by the hunting knife she'd stolen, against the black metal was like music to her ears. And as she stabbed the tires, she imagined the blade was puncturing his black heart.

She returned to the coffee house across the road and took up her earlier position in front of the window with the menu hiding her face. She got to watch Jack's thunderous expression firsthand when he realized his car had been damaged. She hadn't really wanted to hurt him that way, but he needed to learn a lesson and be sorry for what he'd done. Then they could get back together.

Picking up her handbag from off the floor, Claire violently shook the contents onto the bed. A bottle of antipsychotic meds that the doctors prescribed for her because they thought she was a whack job rolled onto the floor. She'd stopped taking them about a month ago, because she didn't believe there was anything wrong. The doctors just wanted her sedated so she couldn't think straight, and so they too could screw with her. Doctor Barlow had also promised to love her, but he'd dumped her when she told the medical staff they were in love and were getting married.

She threw the bottle across the room and watched the tablets spill over the carpet, then she grasped the knife that had created the damage. The light reflected off the silver blade as she held it up to her face.

She probably shouldn't have ruined his stuff, but she'd been so angry and wanted to let him know he couldn't treat her like that. Jack needed to know they belonged together forever.

Lauren drove into her dark driveway. The sensor light above the garage flicked on, illuminating the stairs leading up to her apartment.

Lillian had the apartment built when her boys were teenagers. It gave them the space young men wanted but kept them close enough that she could still keep an eye on them. When they moved out it sat empty for a couple of years before Lillian gave it to Lauren to live in. She often thought she should find an apartment of her own, but she loved her little hideaway above the garage. It was comfortable and had everything she could possibly need, and having Lillian so close was a bonus. They'd often eat dinner together or spend a lazy evening watching TV. She wished Lillian would hurry back from her holiday. She missed her.

Living there also helped her save money, because Lillian considered Lauren a daughter and never asked for much. Anything she saved, she put aside for when Belinda demanded a handout. She knew if she didn't do something to stop Belinda, the woman would eventually suck her dry, but she hadn't worked out how to stop her dirty laundry from being revealed. So, for now, Lauren stayed in her cozy, little apartment above the garage and gave Belinda what she wanted.

The entrance door led straight into the open-plan living room and kitchen she'd decorated in warm colors. Big red and yellow embellished pillows scattered the caramel sofa, and pretty vases and bright bowls—the same as the ones in her store—littered the cream-colored kitchen counter.

Kicking off her heels, she thought about the business card inside her bag, weighing it down like a brick. Heaving the bag off her shoulder, she dropped it onto the glass coffee table. Did she really need to call Jack and accept the job offer so she could pay Belinda? She wished she didn't, but after looking at her bank account, she knew she had no other choice. Which now meant she would have to work closely with a man who made her pulse race and her heart skip a beat whenever he came near. How was she meant to work in such conditions?

Pouring a generous splash of wine, she knocked it back like a shot of whiskey. She'd made an utter fool of herself that morning thinking Jack wanted to ask her out, and now she needed the liquid courage to call him. Lauren poured another glass, not so generously, and sipped it slowly. She sagged into the brown Lazy-Boy chair left behind by Lillian's sons. A chair Ava liked to call the *ugly man chair*. But Lauren didn't care; it was comfortable.

Digging her phone and the business card out of her bag, she dialed Jack's number. Would he gloat when she accepted the job after all? If only she hadn't made such a big song and dance about never working for him. It was going to kill her to bite her tongue and be gracious for the job.

The phone rang twice before Jack answered. "Yes?" His tone was brusque, like she had caught him at a bad time.

After a slight hesitation, she cleared her throat. "Jack, it's Lauren Moore. I'm sorry if I've caught you at a bad time…"

"No, I was just locking up the office." The sharpness in his tone changed, and he sounded like he was happy to hear from her. "What can I do for you, Lauren?"

A magnitude of inappropriate images of what he could do spun through her mind. She shook her head to clear the mental pictures. She needed to stop thinking this way, especially if she was going to work for him.

"I've decided to accept the job offer," she answered, and then, to her horror, realized he may have given it to someone else. He had said he wanted the office fixed urgently. She quickly added, "If it's still available."

"You want the job? Oh, thank freakin' God." His relief was obvious through the phone. "We need to get started right away." He sounded genuinely grateful, and she couldn't detect any smugness. The tension in her body eased a little.

"I could come by the office tomorrow morning to have a look, and we can discuss your tastes and styles."

"I need you to get started sooner than that."

"How much sooner than tomorrow morning can you get?" She laughed.

"We can discuss it over a drink tonight."

With shaky fingers she touched the locket. A drink alone with Jack didn't sound like a great idea, because she needed to keep things purely professional. "No, Jack, I don't think—"

"I can't work the way my office is now, so I'm not taking no for an answer. I'll see you at Jovi's in half an hour." He hung up without waiting for a reply.

Lauren looked at the now silent phone in her hand. Trepidation warned her to stay home and come up with another idea for getting Belinda the money. Because meeting Jack Henderson—the sexy and dangerous football player—for drinks made her stomach do cartwheels. But she reminded herself she was a professional with a job to do, and Jack was merely another client. Something she kept repeating as she freshened up. She ran a brush through her hair, reapplied her apple blossom lip-gloss, and stayed dressed in the white skirt and coral tank top she'd worn to work.

As she put her shoes back on her phone beeped with a text message. Picking it up from the coffee table, she hoped it was Jack texting to cancel their meeting. No such luck.

She opened the text message from Jade.

Thought you might want to see what Mr. Pretty has to offer.

Hubbahubba. If this doesn't turn you on, I don't know what will. J x

Following Jade's message were pictures of Jack in a Calvin Klein campaign, wearing nothing but tighty-whities and come-and-have-sex-with-me eyes. In one photo, he was leaning against a gym wall with a football tucked snugly under his arm. His chest glistened with sweat, his abs washboard hard, and his hooded eyes looked straight into the camera. In the next photo he was lying on a bed with rumpled sheets, with the promise of wanting to do wicked things expressed on his face. Then her gaze zeroed in on the impressive bulge. Surely the photos had been photoshopped? After a thorough inspection, she picked her jaw up off the floor.

The photos were the hottest thing she'd ever seen. They were the kind of photos that made you think of wild, scorching, all-consuming sex, the kind that kept you wanting to go back for more.

Lauren's entire body heated and she wished she had time for a cold shower before heading out to meet Jack. How could she meet him now after seeing him practically naked?

The phone in her hand rang. Startled, she fumbled, almost dropping it on the tiles. Once she had it secure, she answered.

"Did you get the pics?" Lauren could hear Jade's excitement.

"Why did you send me those photos?"

"Aren't they the hottest thing you've ever seen, Lauren?" Yes, they were, but she kept that to herself.

"I saw them in the latest *Cosmo* magazine and thought you needed to see what a stud muffin Jack is. You really need to get your hands on him."

"Jade," she said sternly, hoping to get her point across. "Nothing is going to happen with

Jack. He is not my type, and he does nothing for me." *Liar, liar, pants on fire.* "And it looks like I'm going to be working for him, so it would be extremely unprofessional of me to *get my hands on him.*"

"You're working for Jack? How did that happen?"

Lauren filled her in about Belinda's phone call.

"That bitch. You need to put a stop to her blackmailing. You don't deserve this." Her voice was filled with rage.

Jade, Ava, and Lillian were the only ones who knew how bad it had gotten living with Belinda and Dorothy. They constantly told Lauren not to give Belinda the time of day. But they weren't the ones who would have to live with the consequences once the affair with Graham became public knowledge.

"One day I will," Lauren said to appease Jade. It was a promise she often made but never went through with. Always holding onto hope that Belinda wouldn't come back asking for more money. But after eight years, it didn't seem likely.

"Lauren…" Her friend didn't sound convinced.

"Jade, I will. I need to do it when I'm ready. Listen, I have to go. I'm meeting Jack…" She bit her lip and slapped her forehead. Big mistake letting the meeting with Jack slip. Jade would make a massive deal out of nothing.

"You're meeting Jack?" Jade's voice rose to a high pitch. "This keeps getting better and better."

"Jade, it's for work."

"I hope you're wearing something sexy. Wear your slutty, black dress with the deep V.

Your boobs look fabulous in it."

"Hey, that dress isn't slutty."

"And wear your hair up. Show off that gorgeous neckline you have."

Lauren blew out a breath. "Goodbye, Jade. I'm hanging up."

She pressed the *end call* button in the middle of Jade debating whether she should wear underwear or not.

Chapter 11

$\mathcal{L}$auren took a deep breath and pushed through the heavy timber doors at Jovi's. The blast of music and voices slapped at her as she entered the dim bar, a totally different atmosphere than the subdued Tuesday nights. Fridays brought in the ready-to-party-hard weekend crowd.

Pausing in the doorway, Lauren scanned the pub for Jack but couldn't see him amongst the crowd. She decided to wait for him at the bar and made her way in that direction, pushing through a wall of packed bodies. Soon she found a crack in the crowd and squeezed through to get out of the crush.

A guy with a purple Mohawk and piercings running up both his ears bumped into her and 'accidently' brushed a hand across her butt. She threw him her deadliest look. The one she reserved for guys who got too touchy-feely. He put his palms up and backed away.

Lauren shook her head; Jack was going to be paying

double for his damn new office. Not only did he give her no choice but to meet him tonight, she also had to deal with bodysurfing through a sea of sweaty, over-stimulated guys with wandering hands.

Finally finding a small break, she started to make her way through when a firm hold on her hip stopped her from going any further. She was about to turn around and tell the frisky Mohawk dude he'd better take his filthy fingers off her or she would find somewhere to shove them. But her name, whispered on a sexy, warm breath that teased the sensitive skin below her ear, stopped her in her tracks. She knew exactly who that dreamy voice belonged to.

Turning slowly to face Jack, her gaze dropped to his sexy, white smile. They stood close enough for her to see he had a slightly crooked tooth which only made his smile more devilish and tempting. The desire to taste those lips was a no-go zone, so she flicked her gaze away.

"I didn't know it was going to be so crowded here tonight." He leaned toward her so their chests touched and his lips brushed against her ear as he spoke.

"Yes, it's very crowded," she managed to say as she tried to step away from the penetrating heat of his body only to bump into someone behind her.

"I have a table waiting for us away from the dance floor, but we can leave if you want to go somewhere… quieter?" His breath fanned along her face and neck.

She squirmed from a sudden rush of desire that hit all her good places, and nibbled her bottom lip. The devil tempted her with his smooth-as-sin words.

He pulled back to look at her; his intentions clear in his lusty, emerald eyes.

Why didn't her *Mr. Pretty* aversion work on Jack? If it did, she wouldn't have to worry about going somewhere quieter for their meeting. Because lusty intentions or not, she'd shut it down fast. But when Jack suggested going somewhere quieter, rumpled sheets, white underwear, and come-and-have-sex-with-me eyes filled her mind. Damn Jade for sending those pictures!

Now all she could think about was Jack looking hotter than hell.

They definitely were not leaving Jovi's. The more people around, the better. "Here will be great," she said with a little too much enthusiasm.

He chuckled. The bastard knew he'd rattled her.

She wanted to get this meeting over with so she could go home, open a tub of ice-cream, and forget this day ever happened.

Jack kept a firm hold on her hip, the warmth of his hand searing through the thin fabric of the skirt, as he led them to the same table Lauren and her friends had sat at on Tuesday night. They took a seat at the table. The Corona sign on the wall above their heads buzzed like a bug catcher, and as Jack reached up to tap the sign, his shirt rode up, giving Lauren a peek at a hard stomach. A dark *happy trail* disappeared below the waist of his jeans. Lauren swallowed hard.

The buzzing sign stopped, but the buzzing down in *her* happy place had sprang to life.

She crossed her legs and fanned her face with the drinks menu.

When Jack slid back onto the cracked, vinyl seat a waitress seemed to appear from thin air. Hair bleached the whitest of whites showed black roots, and her makeup had been applied with a heavy hand. A small frame supported a very large chest, and a name-tag, which read Candii with two I's, had been pinned strategically on her double D's. She didn't need the nametag to draw attention to her ample breasts. The tight top and plunging V-neck had them practically spilling out onto the table.

Candii with two I's had her body turned slightly away from Lauren, but she could see the smoldering gaze she gave Jack as she took his order. After ordering a Corona, he asked Lauren what she'd like to drink. Candii turned to Lauren, and the dazzling smile she'd been shining upon Jack dropped like a led balloon. Jealously radiated off the other woman as she trailed a critical gaze up and down Lauren. Sneering at Lauren like she was no competition, Candii waited for her order. Lauren smiled back sweetly, letting her know that the perusal hadn't affected her, and ordered her usual margarita. Giving Jack another flirty smile, Candii promised to be back very soon.

They'd only been sitting there a few minutes when some football fans approached Jack. The guys were excited to see a legend in their bar and wanted to tell him how much they loved watching him play. The girls flirted, ignoring Lauren, and posed for photos. He smiled and laughed with them, took photos, signed autographs, and answered questions about the upcoming season.

When Candii arrived with their drinks, Jack excused himself so he could have a drink with his date. *Date?* This was a business meeting, not a date! Lauren would have said something, but she got distracted by Candii making a production of serving Jack his drink. Slowly bending from the waist, giving Jack a bird's eye view of her abundant breasts, Candii placed a napkin then the Corona on the table. She told Jack if there was anything, *anything* more he wanted to let her know. Lauren was certain she wasn't referring to getting him another drink. Candii went on to serve Lauren's drink with a lot less poise, then she reluctantly left them alone.

Lauren's lips twitched, her annoyance with Jack calling this a 'date' momentarily forgotten.

He watched her over the top of his beer with a raised eyebrow. "What's so funny?"

"Candii, serving you your beer with her boobs." She couldn't hold back the laughter bubbling inside any longer.

Jack swung his head around and glanced over his shoulder in the direction their waitress had gone. "She was? Dammit, I didn't notice," he said, feigning innocence.

Lauren laughed again. Jack couldn't have missed Candii's X-rated attention, but he gave no sign of noticing it. His tongue hadn't rolled out of his head and onto the table like some cartoon character. Nor did he give her ass a once-over when she sashayed away. In fact, most of the women who'd approached him earlier had given him the promise of *a great night* with their eyes, uncaring that

Lauren was sitting at the table looking like she could very well be his date; after all, they didn't know it was only a business meeting. But not once had Jack flirted back like she thought he would. He kept the conversations friendly and polite.

He was probably used to women drooling over him. And he gave them a lot to drool over too. Being rich, famous, and sexy as hell was a great incentive for many women.

But not for Lauren. She reminded herself he was the worst combination for her, and she was there for one reason only—she needed a job.

"So, Jack, about your office…"

"And now it's gone."

"What? The job?" How could the job be gone? Half an hour ago he said it was still available.

Jack shook his head. "Your laugh." His gaze dropped to her lips. "Your sexy smile. For a minute there I thought you'd lightened up and relaxed."

"This isn't a date." She needed to make sure he knew she didn't like his earlier comment.

"Well, with you scowling at me I don't think anyone would believe we're on a date." His eyes sparkled with laughter.

"Good, because this is definitely not one."

"Okay." He looked at her as if he had other ideas.

"It's not. We are here to talk about your office."

Sitting back in the seat, he stared at her with a sexy, crooked grin.

Lauren picked up her purse from the table and slid

across the booth to leave. "Thanks for the drink, Jack, but we should discuss this some other time, preferably at your office during office hours."

Grabbing her wrist, Jack stopped her from leaving. "I'm sorry, Lauren. I was only teasing you."

"If you think coming to this over-populated meat market on a Friday night is fun, think again. I'd rather be home in bed." She knew they were the wrong words to say as soon as they left her mouth. His eyes had lost the playful look and were replaced by a smoky, sexy one. Not wanting to get drawn into them, she needed to move on quickly. "Can we please discuss what you'd like to do with your office so I can go home?"

"I'm glad you decided to take the job." He must have realized she was seriously prepared to leave if he didn't start talking business. "What made you change your mind?"

"My circumstances changed." She took a long drink of her margarita, like the alcoholic liquid could wash away the ugliness of Belinda's phone call.

Her expression must have been grim, because Jack leaned forward and looked at her closely. "Is everything okay?"

"I found out this afternoon my mother had a stroke and I need to help my sister pay for the medical bills." Lauren felt no reason to hide why she needed the money.

"Lauren, I'm so sorry."

With a shake of her head, she stopped his condolences. Words of sorrow meant nothing when she wasn't feeling it herself. Feelings for her mother died the day she left home young, pregnant, and with nowhere to go. Accepting someone's sympathy would make her feel like a fraud.

"It's okay. We weren't close."

The sympathy in his eyes turn to curiosity. Only her closest friends knew about her family. But she decided to tell Jack an abbreviated version of her life so he wouldn't think of her as a heartless bitch.

"I didn't have a typical mother. She didn't love or show affection to her kids. Well, mainly me. She tolerated my sister Belinda, but I was a different story." Jack watched her intently. "I never knew my father. He left a few days after I was born. I wasn't planned, and he never wanted any more kids after Belinda, so he left. My mother blamed his leaving on me."

Lauren gave Jack a brief version of living with Belinda's constant bullying and Dorothy's neglect. His strong, silent presence had her opening up, something she hadn't done for a long time. It hadn't been her intention to tell him so much, but the music and chatter seemed to have dimmed around them and she felt like they were the only two people in the room. She had to hand it to him, not once did he look shocked or repulsed by her family history. Although she'd opened up about her crappy childhood, she couldn't tell him about Belinda's blackmailing. That part of Lauren's life felt dark and dirty.

Anyone taking notice of them would have believed they really were on a date. During her trip down memory lane, Jack had moved over to her side of the booth and held her hand. If Lauren hadn't been in such deep thought she would have snatched it away with a snarky comment about keeping his hands to himself. But the warmth and strength of his touch had soothed the emotions rolling through her when she spoke about her family.

Then the reality of their surroundings and who she was sitting with slowly filled their sanctuary. The music and chatter surrounded them once again, and the false sense of being alone vanished. She slowly slid her hand away from his and immediately missed the warmth.

"I'm sorry you never had the family you deserve. No kid should grow up like that."

Facing him, the closeness unnerved her, and she tried shifting a little on the seat to put some distance between them. The move didn't get her far enough away. "Thanks."

"It must have been tough."

She shrugged off the comment with disregard. "I got over it a long time ago." Jack raised an eyebrow as if questioning whether she was telling the truth.

"So, about your office, do you have any idea what you would like for me to do?" She changed the subject before he asked too many questions. Questions she didn't want to answer.

Not mentioning her subject change, Jack answered, "Everything needs to be done. Walls need repainting, new carpet…the works. Everything got trashed."

"Do you have a color scheme in mind?" Lauren drummed her fingers on the tabletop as ideas sprang to mind.

Shrugging his shoulders, he smiled. "Nope, I'll leave it up to my designer."

"Hmm, I'm thinking maybe pink walls with purple trimmings and white, lacy curtains. How does that sound?" Lauren gave Jack a mischievous grin.

Tapping a finger to his chin, he pretended to look like he was considering it. "The pink and purple walls sound good, but I draw the line at white, lacy curtains."

A laugh bubbled from her. "If you had let me meet you in the morning instead of rushing me out here tonight, I would've brought along a color swatch for you and we could've picked out some colors." Actually, it was Jade's text message that had her forgetting the samples.

"Well now, you'll need to come by in the morning and we can look at colors then."

"So what was the point of this meeting? You could have told me over the phone what you wanted done."

"I used the office as an excuse to take you out for a drink," he answered, not looking at all sorry for misleading her. His fiery gaze traveled over her body, burning her from the inside out.

And that's my cue to leave.

Jack may have tricked her into the meeting, but he definitely wasn't getting anything more. If he thought the rest of the evening was going to consist of less clothing and a lot of heavy breathing, he had another thing coming. She just had to remember who he was—Jack Henderson, football playboy of the century.

Reality hit her in the face like a splash of cold water. It

was only a few days ago he had been there with another woman, and now he thought he could get lucky with her?

She picked up her purse, pushed away from the table, and rose. "Good night, Jack." He wrapped his fingers around her wrist and stopped her once again from leaving.

"What's the rush?"

"We're going to be work colleagues, nothing more. You tricked me into coming here to have a drink with you so you can what…get me to go home with you? I don't work like that, especially when it was only a few nights ago you were here with another woman!" He looked puzzled, and she chuckled with disbelief.

"The tall and gorgeous Amazon queen. Surely you haven't forgotten her already?"

Recognition lit up his face, and he laughed. "Sophia is going to love that description."

Disgusted, Lauren shook her head. "I'm leaving."

"No, no. Wait." His lips were still twitching with laughter. With his hand still wrapped firmly around her wrist he pulled her back down to the seat. She didn't want to cause a scene so she sat back down.

Rubbing her brow, she sighed. "Jack, you're wasting your time with me. I'm not one of those women who'll wait in line for your attention. Do you have a different woman for each night of the week? Amazon queen on Tuesday, some other women for the rest of the week, but had a free spot tonight and thought I could fill it? I'm not interested, Jack."

"She's gay."

"What?"

"Sophia, the Amazon queen, she's gay."

Lauren rolled her eyes. "Do you expect me to believe that? She was all over you like a bad suit." Actually, they had sat and watched sports. She had occasionally touched him gently on the arm or his thigh; not exactly a display of indecent behavior.

"Do I detect a bit of jealousy?" Hope shined from his eyes.

Yes! But instead, she scoffed and waved a hand to dismiss the comment. "Hardly."

He smirked like he didn't believe what she'd said. "She was the Flaming Stars physiotherapist when I was playing footy. Every guy on the team tried hitting on her, but she was never interested. No one could understand it until one day she showed up at a game with her *girlfriend*. Most of the boys cried like babies for days." He chuckled.

"It looked cozy to me." Lauren narrowed her eyes, still unconvinced.

"She's an old friend. She comes out with me some-times and has seen how women can get a little *friendly* around me. So now when we go out for a drink, she pretends that she can't keep her hands off me, and it keeps the groupies away. It works most of the time."

"Must suck to be you." Sarcasm dripped from Lauren's voice.

His full lips tilted up into a smile. "I'm not gonna lie, it used to be a lot of fun, but after years of women throwing themselves at me it got boring."

"I repeat, must suck to be you."

He laughed, the sound so low and sexy it did crazy things to her mind and body—most definitely her body. It was time to leave this place before she turned into one of those women she hated who threw themselves at him.

Looking down at their joined hands, Jack's thumb was now making slow circles on the inside of her wrist. Her nipples peaked and heat ignited between her legs. Yes, he was doing crazy things to her body.

She pulled her wrist free and searched for the nearest exit. "Well, I'm still not interested in anything other than the job." Her traitorous voice wavered and sounded unconvincing.

"Contrary to what you believe, I don't have a different woman for each night of the week." But his alluring green eyes told her he would like her for the night. It was never going to happen. She couldn't allow herself to go there, no matter how attractive and irresistible Jack was.

"Good night, Jack."

This time he didn't stop her from leaving, and disappointment curled in her belly. Damn Jack for doing this to her.

"I'll walk you out," he said as he stood. She opened her mouth to tell him no, but he added, "You don't have a choice. It's late, and there are a lot of idiots around."

She knew he probably wouldn't take no for an answer, so she let him lead her out of Jovi's.

They stepped out into the night, the sky clear and full of stars, and a cool breeze washed over Lauren's body, doing little to douse the heat generating from the man standing inches from her. Nothing but a cold shower, or two, could take care of that problem.

"Thanks for the drink, Jack. I'll come by your office in the morning around eight before I go to work."

He nodded and said, "I'll walk you to your car."

"My car's not far, I can…"

He narrowed his eyes, and the look left her with no other choice but to walk with him.

"Do you always get what you want?" she asked.

"Not always."

Scoffing, she gave him a disbelieving look.

They reached her car and she rummaged through her purse for the keys. "I'm now working for you, you've taken me out for a drink, and you've walked me to my car." The car beeped when she pressed a button on the keys. "I'd say you've gotten everything you wanted from me tonight."

Moving closer, Jack pressed her up against the side of the car. "If I always got what I want, you'd be in my bed right now." His warm lips brushed against her jaw. "So tell me, Lauren, am I going to get everything I want?"

Without waiting for an answer, he pressed his lips firmly on hers. His tongue parted them and, with bold strokes, entered her mouth. A moan involuntarily escaped her. The force of his kiss seared the top of her head and down to the tips of her toes, and every good spot in between.

She hadn't been kissed this good in years.

Strong fingers tunneled their way into her hair, and her body shivered as if icy fingers trailed down her spine.

Knees turning to jelly, she was thankful for the car holding her up. Body taking over from mind, Lauren melted under his mind-blowing touch. As she explored the contours of his chest with her fingertips, his muscles bunched beneath the soft fabric of his shirt.

His lips left her mouth, and she gasped when they found the sensitive spot on the side of her neck. A trail of kisses scorched her skin, and she tilted her neck to the side, giving him better access.

Nibbling below her ear, he whispered on a warm breath, "Come home with me."

Mind foggy from the delicious sensations ravaging through her body, she didn't understand what he was saying.

Probably reading the confusion on her face, he repeated, "Come home with me." Staring into his eyes, she saw her own heavy with lust reflecting from them. "I want you in my bed, not up against a car."

Finally, his words sunk in, and Lauren pulled away. Well, as much as she could with a car behind her. The fog lifted from her mind and she looked around, mortified that someone might be witnessing her slutty behavior. She had been making out with Jack while people walked about and cars drove past. The thought turned her skin cold. How had she let herself get to this point?

"Jack, we're going to be working together. You need to keep your hands to yourself," she snapped. There was no way she'd let him think she was going to be another notch in his belt.

"Looks like you're the one who can't keep your hands

to yourself." He glanced down at her hands still placed on his chest.

Snatching them away, she crossed her arms over her heaving chest. He chuckled low and deep, and even though she was mad as hell for forgetting everything she believed in, goose bumps spread like fire along her skin.

Careful not to touch any part of his body, Lauren slid along the car, and stormed over to the driver's side. "I mean it, Jack, back off."

With a cocky grin, he said, "I told you I don't always get what I want."

Swinging the door open, she slid onto the seat, then slammed the door hard enough to shake the care. When she drove off, she tried hard not to look back at Jack one last time in the rear-view mirror. But dammit, she couldn't help herself.

Chapter 12

$\mathcal{L}$auren pulled into a carpark a few meters down the road from Henderson's Sports, got out of the car, and slipped her sunglasses on. The heat bouncing from the road promised another scorching January day. The pale pink maxi dress she wore had been a good decision. It kept her cool and comfortable. Something she needed to be when she'd be in the same room as Jack, the human fireball.

Grabbing her leather briefcase from the backseat, she locked the car and, on shaky legs, walked the few meters to Jack's office. Last night's kiss played on repeat in her mind, and she didn't know how she was going to face him.

Henderson's was impressive. The building sprawled over the corner of Ocean and Bridge Streets. It was two stories high, sleek and modern, made with lots of glass, chrome, and smooth black surfaces. The name *Henderson's* was illuminated in orange across the top.

Lauren followed the building until she found the entrance to Jack's office. She hesitated. Wiping her clammy hands on her dress, she took a deep breath, pushed the glass door open, and walked into a dark reception area. Behind the reception desk were double timber doors. A gold plaque with Jack's name stamped on it showed her where she might find him.

With a soft knock, she tentatively opened the door and peeked inside. Jack sat at a battered, old table, busily punching away on a laptop. Because he hadn't spotted her, she took the time to try and settle the butterflies flying around inside her stomach. But the more she stood there watching him, the bigger the butterflies grew.

He wore a navy blue polo shirt with a red star surrounded by golden flames on the pocket. The buttons were open and exposed his tanned throat. Her body hummed from the memory of Jack trailing his lips along her own neck. Plenty of men had hit on her before, so what was it about Jack that made her mind turn to mush and her body lose all self-control? Well, whatever it was, she had to lock it up and throw away the key, because she was there for one reason only, and it wasn't to get touchy-feely with the hot-looking ex-football player.

Lauren locked her jelly knees, squared her shoulders, and entered the room. "Good morning, Jack." She was pleased to hear her voice sounded confident and not breathless and lusty.

Whipping his head toward the door, Jack beamed a brilliant smile. His electric smile made her knees threaten to unlock again, but she dug deep for the determination to keep strong.

Pointing to the reception area, she said, "No one was out front. I hope you don't mind me letting myself in."

"Not at all. Ellen, my receptionist, will be in later." His gaze traveled over her. "How are you this morning?"

If he was asking how she was after last night's kiss, she wasn't going there. She didn't even know how she was feeling about it. She decided pretending last night didn't happen was the best way to go, so she simply answered, "Fine, thanks."

He stared at her like he wanted to say more, maybe bring up the kiss, but she didn't give him the chance. Lauren turned her back to him and looked around the office. It was empty expect for the old table and a chair that looked like it had come out of a school's classroom.

The explicit word sprayed on the wall grabbed her attention. "Who did you piss off?"

"What makes you think I pissed someone off?" With a raised brow, she gave him an I'm-not-dumb look.

He responded with a sheepish grin.

"Did you call the police?" Walking around the room, she took photos of the area with her phone.

"Nothing I can prove."

She pulled out a measuring tape from her briefcase and measured the size of the window.

Getting up from the chair, Jack grabbed the other end of the tape to help her.

"She's one pissed off woman," Lauren said while scribbling down measurements on a notepad.

He raised an eyebrow. "How did you know it was a woman?"

The angry red writing said it all. "A man would probably follow you into a dark alley and beat the crap out of you, but a woman…" She waved her arm to take in the office. "…would trash your office and write love letters on the walls."

"Do you know this from experience?" he teased.

No, she'd never done anything like this, but she'd be lying if she said she hadn't thought about getting Graham back in some horrible way.

A woman calling out Jack's name from the reception area saved her from answering.

"I'm in here," he called out.

A pretty lady with light brown hair and tired green eyes entered the room, pushing a dark gray pram. Smiling widely, Jack walked over to the pram and reached inside. The woman slapped his hand away and whispered, "Don't wake her. She's been up all night crying and is absolutely miserable this morning. This is the first sleep she's had in hours."

"What's wrong with her?" Jack peered into the pram with concern.

"Not sure. I'm on my way to see Doctor Sandon. I just stopped in so we can quickly check the order that arrived yesterday afternoon."

"Don't worry about it. We can do it tomorrow." He turned to Lauren. "Leah, have you met Lauren? She's the owner of the shop Mum likes to spend our inheritance at.

She's going to fix my office. Lauren, this is my sister Leah."

Leah's attention had been on her sleeping baby, and she looked surprised to see that there was someone else in the office. "Sorry, I didn't notice you. Hi, Lauren, how are you?"

"Good, thanks," Lauren answered. "How are you?"

"Tired." She laughed. "I didn't slept all night." Dark smudges smeared the bottom of her eyes, and she looked ready to drop. She turned back to Jack. "I'd rather check it now. I don't know what's going on with Emma, so I don't know when I'll get a chance to come back. It won't take long."

"Do you have much more to do here?" Jack asked Lauren.

"I wanted to go over color schemes and the type of furniture you like, but we can do it tomorrow."

"I'll leave that stuff up to you."

"Excellent. So it's the pink and purple color scheme we discussed last night?" she replied, laughing, but it died when he gave her a heated look that had nothing to do with picking color schemes like they'd joked about. She cleared her throat. "Umm… I'll need to take a few more measurements, but you don't need to be here."

Leah, oblivious, or just too tired to notice the sexual tension in the room, laughed. "My brother looks so handsome in pink." She glanced down at the sleeping baby and frowned. "I thought Ellen might have been here to watch Emma. She might wake up with the noise in the storeroom." Then she stared at Lauren and nibbled her bottom lip, looking like she was trying to assess her character. Glancing back down at the sleeping baby, she appeared to have made a decision. "You wouldn't mind looking after Emma for a few minutes, would you, Lauren?"

The request had Lauren's gaze darting to the pram, and she reached for her locket. She couldn't see the sleeping baby inside, nor did she want to. "Umm… I wasn't going to be here much longer."

"We'll be quick, I promise. I don't want to have to make another trip back." With pleading eyes, she continued. "She really needs to sleep before the doctor starts poking at her."

The poor woman looked desperate. How could she say no? "Okay," she said on a whisper.

Blowing out a long breath, Leah's shoulders sagged with relief. "You're wonderful. Quick, Jack, let's go." And she ran out of the office.

Jack studied Lauren's face with concern. It was as if he knew something wasn't quite right. "Will you be okay?"

The reassuring smile she tried to give him wobbled. "Sure."

Jack didn't look convinced. "We won't be long," he assured her and followed Leah from the room.

Lauren didn't know how long she stood frozen. She avoided babies as much as possible. Never looked at them, and definitely never touched them. After tragically losing her own the pain of being near a small, delicate, innocent little being sliced through her heart like thousands of tiny knives, so she learned to avoid them completely.

When mothers came into the store with their babies it

was Jaime who assisted them. Lauren always found something urgent to do, either back in her office or outside the shop. The smaller the baby, the harder it was to deal with.

A soft mewling sound snapped Lauren out of her daze and drew her attention to the pram. She looked at it like a giant, human-eating spider was about to crawl out of it. She had a better chance dealing with one of those than she did a tiny baby.

The sounds soon turned into loud whimpers, but Lauren still couldn't move. Her gaze flicked to the office door, and she prayed Leah would be back at any second. But Leah didn't come back and Emma's cries grew louder and more insistent, and Lauren could see her tiny hand flailing above the edge of the pram. The cries grew more frantic and urgent, and Lauren had no choice but to go over to her.

With trepidation she peered into the pram. The screaming bundle was wrapped in a white muslin cloth with tiny pink and yellow flowers delicately sewn into the light fabric. Both arms had broken free of the wrap and waved agitatedly above her head. Fuzzy, soft wisps of brown hair covered her head, and a pink elastic headband with a butterfly attached was slipping from her head. The baby scrunched up her face, which was red with distress, and two tiny, glistening tears shimmered from her dark blue eyes.

Lauren's hands shook as she reached inside the pram, like she was putting them into the cage of a lion. Softly, she patted Emma's stomach and whispered, "Ssshhh."

But her pathetic attempt at comforting was useless, and it only made the crying louder.

All she could think to do to stop Emma from fussing was pick her up. The thought turned Lauren's blood ice cold, but what other choice did she have? She couldn't let her keep crying like this.

Slowly and gently, she slipped her hands under the fretting baby, one supporting the head and one under the bulging nappy, and with awkward hands, lifted Emma into her arms. She walked over to the only chair in the office and sat, bouncing her arms slightly. As Lauren stared down at the crying baby, her mind drifted to another time when she held a baby in her arms: a silent, lifeless baby.

Lauren lay limp on the hospital bed, sucked of all energy. According to the silver clock on the wall, she'd been in labor for seven long hours and didn't think she could last much longer. But Jess, her midwife, had encouraged her by telling Lauren it was time to start pushing. Propping herself up on her elbows, she gritted her teeth, and with the little energy she could muster, pushed.

Moments later Jess looked at Lauren with concern stamped on her face. "Honey, I need you to stop pushing."

"What's wrong?" Lauren asked when Jess shouted out orders to another nurse in the room.

"Just relax, honey. I need a little help." Jess smiled, but the concern in her eyes told another story. When Jess told the

nurse to call the doctor right away Lauren knew something was terribly wrong.

A short, balding man with a gray beard and round stomach rushed in, snapping on latex gloves as he approached and exchanged whispered words with the midwife.

Lauren's heart raced, and she tried to sit up. "What's happening? Is there something wrong with my baby?"

The doctor turned to her with an ominous expression. "Your baby's cord is wrapped around its neck. We need to work as fast as possible to free it."

Terror traveled like an out-of-control train up her spine. "Will she be okay?" Deep in her heart she'd always known the baby was a girl.

"We're doing everything we can," he said, positioning himself between her legs.

"Please don't let anything happen to her," she cried.

"Lauren, we need you to lie down and stay as calm as possible," Jess soothed.

The next few minutes Lauren did exactly what she was told. She no longer felt the pain and exhaustion of labor. The worry in her heart was a thousand times worse.

After a few more pushes and one last guttural scream, the baby was born, and Lauren struggled to sit up. She wanted to see her baby, but the doctor whisked her away to a corner of the room before she got the chance.

Why wasn't her baby crying?

"I want to see my daughter!" Panic laced her words.

No one answered her. Fear gripped her heart and wouldn't let go. She swung her legs off the bed, determined to get to her baby, but Jess stopped her.

Lauren pushed Jess's arms away. "Why isn't she crying?"

Jess placed a hand on Lauren's shoulder. "She's not breathing. The doctor is doing everything he can to help her."

Not breathing? "No-no-no." Lauren shook her head, not wanting to believe what she was hearing. "Please help her," she pleaded on a sob as she watched the medical staff frantically work on her baby. "Please, please, please breathe, my baby girl."

She wrapped her arms around her waist as harsh sobs shook uncontrollably through her body.

Lauren didn't know how long she kept pleading for her precious baby to breathe. But when the efforts of the staff stopped and the doctor looked up at the silver clock, she screamed, "Nooo! Don't stop. Please don't stop. Make her breathe." The doctor's mournful face stared back at her. "Please," she said on a broken whimper.

He shook his head. "I'm so sorry. We couldn't save her. We did everything we could."

"Oh God!" Lauren collapsed on the bed as the pain ripped through her body. Jess tried to console her, but it was just a jumble of meaningless words.

The doctor placed a hand on her arm. "I'm truly sorry for your loss. The nurses will bring her over to you."

A nurse placed her baby, wrapped in a pink hospital blanket, into the cradle of her arms, and she gazed down at her beautiful girl with her precious, unmarked face. Her tiny lips, which were tinged blue, were slightly open, and her eyes were closed. She looked like she was sleeping.

"Wake up," she pleaded as she shook the precious bundle. Her head, covered in soft, light brown fuzz, lolled to the side.

Violent sobs raked through Lauren's body as she wept for her lost child.

She placed kisses on her cheeks, eyes, mouth, and the top of her little head. Then she counted every perfect finger and kissed each one. Lauren's fingers caressed her soft face and the velvety folds of skin around her neck. Carefully placing her silent baby on the bed, she unwrapped her and counted her toes and touched her chubby little legs. Her skin felt smooth, soft, and cold. Lauren quickly wrapped her back up and rubbed her tiny hands in her own. When she couldn't warm them she asked Jess for another wrap.

"I don't think it's necessary," Jess answered with care.

"She's cold, get her another wrap," Lauren snapped.

Jess nodded and rushed off to retrieve one.

When she came back, she handed Lauren a blanket, and she wrapped her baby in it. "There you go, sweetheart. Mummy will warm you up," she crooned as she rocked her baby gently in her arms.

She held her baby for hours, burning her face into her memory. When it was time to let her go, tears poured down Lauren's face like warm rivers and fell into her baby's closed eyes, looking like her own tears, tears she should have shed a hundred times in her life.

She kissed her one last time with all the love she had and all the love she would always have, and whispered, "I'll love you forever, Abby."

Emma's loud cries pulled her from the past and back to the present. Pain that had become less stabbing over the years roared fierce and strong through her, and Lauren found it difficult to discern reality. This was not Abby, it was Emma.

Emma put an angry fist in her mouth and sucked, quietening down for a moment, but then spat it out and the wailing began again. Lauren spotted a yellow dummy in the pram so she got up to get it then put it into Emma's mouth. Emma suckled the dummy and looked up at

Lauren with big, blue, watery eyes, and Lauren, not for the first time, wondered what color Abby's eyes would have been.

Lauren gently rocked her in her arms as Emma rhythmically sucked on the dummy. Emma's wide eyes soon grew heavy and drooped closed. The sucking stopped, her mouth grew slack, and the dummy slipped from her lips. Lauren felt the blood drain from her body and her knees turn to water. Horror gripped at her heart.

Emma had stopped breathing.

Chapter 13

ack entered his office with Leah and found Lauren looking panicked and as white as a sheet.

Racing over to them, Lauren cried, "She's not breathing!"

"What?" Leah's eyes grew wide, and she grabbed Emma from Lauren's arms.

Wrapping her arms around her stomach, Lauren bent at the waist. Jack thought it wouldn't be long before she crumbled in a heap on the floor, so he placed soothing hands on her shoulders and straightened her up. She uncontrollably shook in his arms.

"What happened?" he asked, ducking his head to search her face.

"When you left, she started to cry so I picked her up, and she stopped breathing."

Emma got jostled awake when passed between Lauren and Leah. Howling her displeasure at being woken. Jack glanced over his shoulder at Emma. "Lauren, she's fine." "She's breathing?" Lauren didn't sound convinced.

This time Leah answered. "I think she's making enough noise to prove it." She gave Lauren a soothing smile.

"Oh, thank God." Lauren's shoulders sagged as Jack led her to the chair. He sat her down and she dropped her head in her hands.

Catching Jack's attention, Leah raised a questioning eyebrow. Shrugging, he nodded toward the door. Leah took it as her cue to leave.

"Lauren, look at me." Jack placed a hand on her back and squatted down beside her.

"What happened?"

She took a deep breath, and Jack felt it shudder through her. "I thought she stopped breathing."

"She fell asleep."

"I didn't know that." Lifting her head, she looked at him with panicked eyes, her face still drained of all color.

"Why would you think she had stopped breathing?" He rubbed circular motions on her back, trying to calm her.

"Because that's what babies do." Her shaking hand reached for the locket around her

neck. He had seen her fiddle with it many times and realized she did so when uncomfortable or stressed.

Jack grabbed her cold hands and rubbed them to try to get some warmth back into her. Her body still trembled, and sadness was etched on her chalk-white face.

There had to be something big going on. "Lauren, you can talk to me."

Her eyes held his as if they were her lifeline. Hurt shot through his chest for the unspoken pain spilling from them.

On a whisper that was barely audible, she said, "I had a baby girl."

Jack's stomach dropped to the floor. He knew whatever she was about to say wasn't going to be good.

"She was born with the cord…" Her voice cracked, and he held her hands tighter. "They couldn't save her. I'd never seen anything so beautiful and so perfect, but she wouldn't breathe.

She looked like she'd fallen asleep in my arms."

"Arrh, fuck. Come here, honey." Pulling her up onto her unsteady feet, he sat on the chair, pulled her down onto his lap, and cradled her like a toddler.

She took a deep, shuddery breath, which vibrated against his chest, then told him about her affair with Graham Stone and his rejection after she fell pregnant. And how she found out he was married after seeing his picture in a magazine with his beautiful wife and their brand-new baby.

Needing to offer comfort, his arms tightened around her. He couldn't imagine the pain she must have gone through. "I'm so sorry, honey." Brushing her hair back from her pale face, he looked into her eyes. The black, spikey lashes surrounding them made the gold flecks shine bright. He brushed a tear from her cheek. "If I had known, I never would've let Leah leave Emma with you."

"I over-reacted—"

He placed a light, feathery kiss on her lips, stopping her from saying any more.

"Sshh, no honey, I'm sorry," he whispered as his lips connected again with hers.

Jack hadn't planned on kissing her, though he'd been thinking about it ever since the night before. Not wanting to take advantage of her in such a fragile and vulnerable state, he tried to hold back. But as she sat curled up on his lap, looking so sad, he wanted to take the grief from her eyes so he kissed her.

Any second now he was going to stop.

But when Lauren moaned low in her throat and clutched her fists in his shirt, he couldn't have stopped if he tried. Sliding his tongue into her mouth, Jack deepened the kiss. The sweet taste of her was like the richest honey.

The hold she had on his shirt loosened, then she clung to his shoulders as she pressed her body against his chest. A surge of lust slammed into him like a one-hundred kilo fullback going in for a tackle. And he needed to feel more of her. Lifting her, he twisted her around so she straddled him. The evidence of his lust pressed against her pert butt, which fit snug on his lap.

She inhaled sharply in response, and he knew she was just as affected.

Lauren rocked enthusiastically against him. Jack sucked in a sharp hiss and placed his hands on her hips to keep her still. He'd never been this turned on in his life, and if she continued to rock, he'd be ending things in his pants.

Cupping her face in his hands, he met her hot gaze. Her golden eyes burned bright. Her cheeks were flushed red, and her pink mouth was swollen from his kisses. Pride at putting the just-been-kissed-real-good expression on her face made his chest expand.

The need to see more of her was so strong. His hands shook as he removed them from her face to slide the thin straps of her dress down her arms. As he trailed a finger along the tops of her breasts, she shivered, and her chest rose and fell rapidly at his touch. To help control his own racing heart, he took a deep, shuddery breath. God, he wanted her so bad.

With nimble fingers he flicked the clasp at the front of her bra and released her breasts. White, firm perfection with rosy tips fit perfectly in his hands. Lowering his head, he placed a kiss on a raised peak.

A sigh of pure pleasure left Lauren's mouth. Her head fell back and she arched her spine, pressing herself closer to his mouth. "Oh God… Jack…"

Taking that as his cue, he lingered over her breasts. Damn, they were so beautiful. He could sit there all day paying tribute to them, but the hunger coiled in his gut grew stronger and he wanted even more.

Jack slid his palms up her legs and bunched her dress around her waist. The soft, sighing sounds she made drove him wild. He slid a finger under the elastic of her undies and found her warm center. Jerking at the touch, she cried out. Loving how sensitive she was, he urged her to rock against his hand while he feasted on her breasts. Jack worked another finger in, and she rocked faster, her breath coming out in little gasps.

"Oh God, Jack… I'm going to…"

"Let go, honey." His own body quivered with the need for release.

Lauren shuddered around him and collapsed with a cry of pleasure on his chest.

While she got her breathing under control, Jack held her. When her body stiffened in his arms, he knew the realization of what just happened had sunk in.

Lauren pulled away from him with wide eyes and fumbled with the clasp on her bra. She slid the straps of her dress back into place and lifted herself from his lap as clumsily as someone with two left feet.

"Jack, this shouldn't have happened." Turning her back to him, she straightened out her clothes.

"It seems to me like we can't help ourselves."

Swinging back around to face him, she frowned. "You need to stay away from me."

Jack rose and took a step toward her. She took one back and held up her hand like a stop sign.

"I mean it, Jack. When you get too close funny things start happening inside me, and my brain turns stupid and I can't control myself."

"Sounds like you should shut that brain of yours off now and then, and let your body do the thinking," he said, trying to lighten the mood, because she looked as skittish as a newborn foal.

"I don't know why it doesn't work with you." She

placed her hand on her forehead like she was checking for a temperature. "It's always worked before."

Jack had no idea what she was talking about. "What doesn't work?"

"I'm not supposed to even *notice* you."

Again, he had no clue what she meant. "Why?" he asked with confusion.

"Because you're a *Mr. Pretty*, that's why." She dug her hands on her hips and rolled her eyes like it was something he should understand.

If he hadn't felt a strong pull of attraction, he might have gone running for the door, silently screaming 'crazy woman', but instead, he slowly said, "I'm a *Mr. Pretty*?"

"Yes." She blew out a breath.

"Am I supposed to know what that is?"

She paced in front of him. "You're good-looking...great-looking actually. You're wealthy and you're famous. They are all the characteristics of a Mr. Pretty."

"And that's a bad thing?" So there was some truth in what his mother had told him. But he still didn't understand why it was a problem. Women loved that about him.

"Yes, that's a bad thing." Shaking her head, annoyance flickered across her face.

Well and truly confused now, Jack blew out a long, frustrated breath. "You need to explain in simple sentences, for the dummies in the room, why those characteristics are bad."

Lauren stopped pacing and stared at him like *he* was the crazy one. "After Graham, it was like something inside me broke, and I've never noticed anyone like him again. Then you come barging into my shop, and *bang*, there you are, all big and sexy with everything I don't want in a man."

Jack ran his fingers through his hair. "So, let me get this straight. You've had a bad experience with one man, and as a result, all men who may appear to be like him don't register on your radar?" Then he remembered what his mother also said about Lauren on New Year's Eve. She'd mentioned how Lauren went for the 'nerds'. Well, that was Jack's description anyway.

"Yes, and now you've broken it." She actually looked pissed at him.

"I'm glad I have. I'm sorry about what that jerk did to you and what you had to go through, but seriously, you think all men who are successful and good-looking are going to screw you over like Graham?"

"I know it probably doesn't make sense to you—"

"It sure as hell doesn't."

She frowned. "But it's the way it is. I'm going to have to fix it, and by 'fix it', I mean stay away from you."

"Good luck doing that. You work for me now."

She nibbled her lip, and it looked like she was trying to think of a way around the problem. "Well, we can conduct most of it by phone and email."

"Lauren, there's nothing wrong with doing something about this attraction."

"Everything is wrong about it."

"Why?" he asked.

"Because…because… It just is. It needs to stop."

"Honey, fireworks like that don't go off for just anyone," he said, moving closer to her.

"Why would you stop something that we both know would be amazing?"

She bit her bottom lip, drawing his gaze to her plump, full mouth. The urge to taste her again was strong.

"Haven't you been listening? You're not my type." Uncertainty crossed her features, as if she wasn't sure she still meant it.

He could see the quick rise and fall of her chest as he got even closer. "Honey, you were rocking on my lap like I was exactly your type."

Lauren's mouth dropped opened, and a red splash of color stained her cheeks. "This is exactly why you are not my type." Clenching her fists by her sides, she took a couple of steps away from him. "You pretty boys with your good looks and everything else you have, think you can have anyone you want. But I've had my disaster like you, and I have no intention of repeating it just because you're good with your hands."

Now it was Jack's turn to see red, and fury bubbled in his chest. "Hang on a minute.

You're comparing me to the married prick that dumped you after getting you pregnant?"

Her eyes darted away, and she had the good sense to look guilty. "I'm sure you're not exactly like Graham, but men in your league think they can do whatever they want with whoever they want and then move on. I don't want to get involved with someone like that again."

Leaning his hip on the edge of the old table, he folded

his arms across his chest. The casual stance belied the steel in his voice. "You keep judging me on another guy's behavior. It's really pissing me off."

"Look around you, Jack." She opened her arms out wide. "What did you do to this woman to make her come here and trash the place?" When he stood stone silent, Lauren scoffed.

"You may not be as different from Graham as you think you are."

With that, she marched past him to head to the door. Shooting his hand out, he grabbed her arm and pulled her back to face him. "You don't know me well enough to compare me. I'm not seducing a young woman, pretending I'm single and promising things I'm never going to give. This is what it is. Two people finding enjoyment with one another. It doesn't have to be anything more." But a niggling feeling in the pit of his gut tried to tell him something different.

He pushed it away to examine at another time.

"You may be up-front about what you want, but I know enough about you to know

you're not what I want. I've heard about the different women every night, the groupies you pick up, and the sex parties you throw. I also know not to believe everything I hear, but tell me, Jack, is none of that true?"

Dropping her arm, he dug his hands into the pockets of his jeans. He couldn't deny it, because some of what she said was true.

She met his gaze. "I'm not going to be the flavor of the day." She picked up her briefcase and walked toward the door. This time he let her go. "I've got everything I need for now. I'll be in touch when I have something to show you."

Jack stared at the numbers swimming around on the computer screen, not making sense of anything. The more he sat there punching in numbers, the messier he made the spreadsheet. He needed something more physical to do, so he left Ellen to take care of the office and went searching for things to do in the store. Jack tackled through boxes of stock, rearranged exercise equipment, and surprised a few browsing fans.

Even keeping himself busy, he couldn't get Lauren out of his head. The way her stricken face exuded pure fear when she ran to him with Emma was something he'd never forget. If he'd known, he never would have left her alone with Emma.

Then, after she'd gotten off on him, giving him a sweet taste of her and making him want to go back for more, she went and compared him to that prick Graham Stone.

The scumbag had a lot to answer to for letting a young woman go through that kind of hell. Jack never liked him. He always came across as an arrogant asshole who thought his shit didn't stink. A big shot journalist who could interview anyone he wanted, except for Jack. Over the years, on numerous occasions, Graham had requested an interview with Jack, and each time, he refused. He knew Graham didn't want to show Australia the real Jack Henderson. The Jack Henderson who'd worked his butt off to become one of the best football players in the country.

No, Graham was only interested in Jack's social life: the partying and the women.

And now Jack well and truly knew how much of a bastard Graham Stone was. The thought of Lauren, so young and alone, dealing with such a devastating time in her life made his chest tight. So he'd comforted her the only way he knew how. He'd never meant for it to go as far as it did, but when Lauren became so responsive to a couple of kisses there was no stopping him.

Touching her made him hard and ready in a flash. The sweet scent and smoothness of her skin drove him crazy. She'd been so sensitive that she'd exploded like a wildcat on his lap. Jack had to grit his teeth and sing the national anthem in his mind to stop himself from having his own explosion.

Then she had the nerve to tell him he wasn't her type. Not her type? He'd like to see how she reacted to someone who *was* her type. No, wait… That thought made him very uncomfortable. He didn't want to think about Lauren getting her rocks off with another man. Which was stupid really...why should he care? He liked Lauren, liked her a lot, but there was some truth in what she'd said. Jack liked the company of many women, not a different woman every night like she accused him of, but he didn't do the settling-down-with-one-woman thing.

Maybe it was for the best he stayed away from Lauren.

Keep things professional. He wasn't what she needed in her life. She needed more than a quick fuck on a desk chair. But now that he'd gotten a taste of her he couldn't help from wanting to take a bigger bite. Between them, a spark had been lit that promised to build into a dangerous wildfire if not contained.

He needed a damn fire brigade to help him out.

Chapter 14

*L*ater that evening Lauren, Jade, and Ava were having a girl's night in at Ava's unit overlooking Brimland Point beach. The unit reflected Ava's style—modern, sleek, and not a thing out of place. These nights were kept casual, and Lauren and Jade had dressed similarly in denim shorts and tank tops, but Ava's idea of casual was black, painted-on tights and a white and black striped, strapless, clingy top that enhanced her already decent-sized breasts. A pair of pink, fluffy, high-heeled slippers was also her way of dressing down.

"How was your *date* with Mr. Pretty last night?" Jade asked. "Did you wear the slutty black dress like I told you to?" Excitement lit her eyes.

"What's this about a date?" Ava paused with the wine bottle above her glass.

"Lauren and Jack went on a date last night," Jade informed Ava.

"I did not—"

"Ooooh, a date with Jack," Ava interrupted. "Please tell me he was good. I want all the juicy details." She resumed pouring the wine, then sat back and made herself comfortable.

"It wasn't a date. And God, Ava, I didn't sleep with him!" But it had been extremely tempting.

"Shame." Ava took a sip of Chardonnay and looked bored.

"So how did it go? Did you discuss business or did you discuss *getting down* to business?" Jade wiggled her eyebrows.

Lauren averted her eyes and picked a non-existing piece of fluff off her top.

Jade blinked in surprise. "You really did get down to business!"

"You did?" Ava sat straight up in the seat like she found the conversation interesting again.

Lauren couldn't lie to them even if she tried. They could always see straight through her. "Jack kissed me." Reaching for the coke bottle on the table, she poured some into her glass. She was sticking to non-alcoholic beverages, because she didn't need another loose-tongue moment.

"Mr. Pretty," Ava said slowly. "The football star who Jade wanted to be the father of her children kissed you?"

Jade stuck her tongue out at Ava then shoved a handful of peanuts in her mouth.

Ava blew Jade a kiss.

"Uh-huh." Lauren tried to sound like it was nothing. "Don't make a big deal about it. It was only a couple of kisses." She bit her tongue the second she realized what she'd said. Alcohol or not, she still had a big mouth.

Jade's mouth fell open.

"You might want to close your mouth, Jade," Lauren said. "A mouthful of nuts is disgusting."

"Not from my experience," Ava mumbled underneath her breath.

Jade's eyebrows disappeared into her hairline, but she didn't comment on Ava's crude remark. "A couple of kisses! That's more than one. So how many times did you kiss Jack?"

"Aren't you a primary school teacher? You should know a couple means two," Lauren said.

Waving a hand in the air, Jade said, "I know how to count."

"Really? It doesn't seem like it," Lauren teased.

Jade narrowed her eyes at Lauren. "Stop changing the subject and tell us about Mr. Pretty and his fabulous kisses."

Succumbing to what would most likely be questions fired at her, Lauren sighed, curled her legs underneath her, and got comfortable. It could be a long night. "We met for drinks, he walked me to my car, and then he kissed me. See? No big deal." Reaching for the bowl of chips and placing it on her lap, she scooped out a handful and shoved them in her mouth so she didn't have to talk to her nosey friends.

"No way," Jade said, shaking her head. "You're not going to stop there."

Pointing to her lips, Lauren shrugged as if to say

'sorry, can't talk with my mouth full'. But Jade and Ava both crossed their arms over their chests and gave her a look that said they could wait.

After swallowing the chips, Lauren blew out a long breath. "What more is there to say?"

"Was it fantastic?" Jade's eyes looked dreamy.

"Did he cop a feel? Or better yet, did you?" Ava asked as she kicked off her fluffy slippers and tucked her feet under her like she was getting ready to hear a fairy tale. More like she wanted to hear a *kinky* fairy tale.

No, he hadn't that night, but she had. God, she'd never forget how strong his chest felt beneath her hands. Jade squirmed in the chair like an excited puppy, and Ava draped an arm over the back of the couch as they waited for her to answer the questions, but Lauren kept her lips sealed.

Blowing out a frustrated breath, Jade said, "Okay, you won't talk, so let me try to figure this out for myself." Placing a thumb and forefinger on her chin, she tapped a finger. "He walked you to your car and kissed you. But you said he kissed you a couple of times. So do you mean he kissed you once, stopped, and kissed you again?"

Lauren shrugged, picked up the remote control for the TV, and flicked through the channels, trying not to give anything away.

"That's a 'no' then. So, he got in the car with you and you drove to a secluded location and he kissed you again."

"And you did it in the backseat of your car like a couple of horny teenagers," Ava chirped in with excitement.

Lauren rolled her eyes. She couldn't help but laugh at the two trying to figure out what had gone on. She decided to put them out of their misery; they'd eventually get it out of her anyway.

"He kissed me again in his office this morning." She went on to explain what had happened with Emma, how she told Jack about Abby, and how he comforted her while she fell apart. "So he was only comforting a crazy woman the best way he knew how."

"Giving you a hug is being comforting, but putting his tongue down your throat is saying he wants to do the nasty with you," Ava commented.

She wasn't going to tell Ava she was spot-on, so instead she played the denial card. "He doesn't want to do the—"

"Of course he does," both girls said.

Lauren shook her head. "It's not going to happen. I'm not interested." If she said it out loud a few hundred times, she might start believing it.

Ava scoffed and Jade rolled her eyes.

"What?" Lauren asked, exasperated.

"Honey, since Graham you have never let a good-looking guy kiss you. And yet you've let Jack, the stud muffin, kiss you not once but twice," Ava pointed out.

"So?"

"So, if you weren't interested, there's no way in hell you would have let him kiss you." Ava picked up her wineglass and raised it like a toast.

"He caught me by surprise." Even to her ears it sounded unbelievable.

She rose from the sofa and walked over to the window overlooking the beach. It had grown dark and only the lights on the cargo ships were visible in the distance.

Why had she let Jack kiss her at Jovi's and then again in his office? That time the kiss had gone a lot further. Lauren tried to convince herself that she'd needed the comfort, but she knew she was only kidding herself. God, she thoroughly enjoyed it. It was the best orgasm of her life, and they hadn't even had sex.

It had been years since she let anyone like Jack get that close. Her aversion to *Mr. Prettys* must have been understood because it kept them away, and if any were more determined, she shot them down with extra-strength refusal.

The rare times she did date, the men were less than desirable. Sure, they could be a little strange sometimes. One had lived at home with his mum—he was thirty-five. Another was a tortured poet who claimed to have no money because his poems never sold. And the last guy she dated, the Pee-Wee Herman look-alike, was a computer game freak. They were safe because Lauren never needed to worry about having her heart broken by them.

Not for the first time she wondered *why Jack?* Could it be because it had been so long since she'd had sex and her vibrator couldn't replace the touch of a red-hot man? That could explain why she gave Jack a private lap dance. Maybe before she saw Jack again she'd spend some extra time with her battery-operated friend, in the hopes it would take the edge off and stop her from turning into melted butter in his hands. Because even though she told him to stay away and keep his hands to himself, she wasn't completely sure she really wanted him to. And that scared the hell out of her.

"Lauren!" Jade snapped her fingers, getting her attention.

She twisted around to see two sets of impatient eyes staring back at her.

"Why did you let him kiss you?" Jade asked. They weren't going to let this go. "Maybe it's because it's been a while and he was available," Lauren answered.

"Nuh-uh, not buying it." Ava shook her head, her silky, black hair swinging with the movement, but almost immediately it fell perfectly back into place. "It's always 'been a while' and you've *never* let that happen before. And there are always guys available."

Lauren threw her hands in the hair. "He's hot, and I'm horny. That's why. There, happy?"

Blinking in surprise, Ava and Jade paused for a beat, then broke into hysterical laughter, clutched their stomachs, and rolled around on the sofa.

Lauren dug her hands on her hips. "I'm glad this is so amusing."

"Oh God," Ava said, wiping at the tears rolling down her face. "Next time warn us when you're going to use *hot* and *horny* in the same sentence." This brought on more laughter.

Huffing out a breath, Lauren crossed her arms and waited for the laughter to die down. It took a while.

"Okay, okay, I've stopped now. Whew." Jade gasped,

trying to catch her breath, and fanned her face with her hand. "I realize the situation is serious."

"No, it's not—"

Jade held up a hand, stopping Lauren's words. "Yes, it is. Apart from being *hot and horny*."

Jade's lips twitched, but she held it together. Ava, on the other hand, cracked up again.

Lauren picked up a pillow from the sofa and threw it toward her head.

"I'm sorry. I promise I'll behave," Ava said as she blocked the missile.

Lauren doubted Ava could ever behave.

"You let him kiss you *twice*," Jade said.

God, if only they knew what else she'd let him do.

"You wouldn't do that if you didn't feel something for him." Jade's eyes flicked over to Ava's grinning face.

"Oh yeah, she's feeling *horny!*" Ava giggled, and they both rolled around, laughing again.

"This is hopeless. I'm going home." Lauren snatched up her wallet and keys from the glass coffee table.

"No, don't go." Ava grabbed her wrist and tugged her back down to the sofa. "We'll be good, promise." She crossed her heart and smiled like the Cheshire Cat.

Lauren couldn't blame them for their questions and teasing; it really was a big deal to them. To her too. But she didn't understand her attraction to Jack, and she wasn't sure she wanted to. Everything had been going well for her until he came bursting onto the scene. Wasn't it? She had great friends and a job she loved, what more could she want? So what if, in the middle of the night, she would have liked a warm body to snuggle with and a familiar face to wake up to in the morning? Or someone to talk about her day with. Okay, at times she felt a little lonely, but that didn't mean she wanted Jack to fill the void. He was the last person she needed in her life. He would never be long-term.

Ava tried very hard to sober up, but her lips still curled up at the corners in a smile. "Why can't you let yourself be open to the possibility of things going further with Jack?"

Lauren pointed a finger at Jade. "You of all people know what Jack's like. You've relayed dozens of stories about all the women he hooks up with. I don't want to be another one of those women."

Jade, no longer laughing, said, "I don't believe half the stuff I read. I know most of it is rubbish."

"He's admitted there's an ounce of truth in there somewhere. And I'm not interested in being his next conquest."

"You said it's nothing serious," Ava added.

"It's not."

"Well, if it's nothing serious, why can't you have a bit of fun with him? Who cares if he changes women like he changes his undies? You could use some hot, hunky guy to get your motor running for when you're ready to get serious with the real deal." Ava paused then added,

"Unless, you think it could lead to more than just having fun?"

"No," Lauren denied. "I'm not worried about that."

She knew Jack wasn't a forever kind of man. He even

told her he only wanted to have fun. One-night stands were more his thing, and he would be long gone before the sun rose the next day. She wasn't wired that way. Sex had to be more than a heated attraction.

Yes, she was attracted to him. Yes, he was the first *Mr. Pretty* she had noticed since Graham, and yes, he made her feel some weird and wonderful things all through her body. But she knew never to risk handing over her heart to a man like Jack. Nope. Never. Ever. Her body, on the other hand, may be another problem all together. It buzzed with excitement and heat every time he entered a room. No, she would be strong and would put up super-strong, industrialstrength barriers to stop herself from climbing all over him.

Lauren looked at Jade and Ava, her lips twitching, and she buried her face in her hands.

"Did I really say he's hot and I'm horny?"

The sound of hysterical laughter filled the room.

Chapter 15

It had been four days since Jack had seen Lauren. During that time she'd sent him a bunch of emails regarding paint colors, furniture ideas, and times for when workers would be at the office. And Jack did not reply to any of them. Call him childish, but he refused to do business through emails, no matter how uncomfortable she felt being in the same room with him. She would have to face him sooner or later.

Even though he was annoyed with her for avoiding him, her latest email made him laugh. She'd informed him that because he hadn't returned any of her emails regarding colors, the painters had been instructed to go ahead and paint the office purple and pink as previously discussed. An order of white, frilly curtains were also on their way.

He didn't regret kissing her, and if she'd stopped acting pissed off, she'd be able to admit she damn well enjoyed it too.

He hired her to decorate his office, and dammit, she needed to stop hiding behind a computer screen and get her sweet ass over there to do it. As if he'd conjured her up, she came storming into the office, looking fiery and ready for a fight.

This morning she'd dressed in a tight, black skirt with a white top with black-capped sleeves. Her honey silk hair hung in waves down her back. She was the sexiest thing he'd ever seen, even with the scowl she wore.

"Good morning, Lauren. Nice of you to finally show up for work." He leaned back in the chair, put his feet up on the old, scarred table, and took a sip of his morning coffee.

Lauren dropped her briefcase hard on the desk and snapped, "You haven't answered any of my emails."

"I know," he said with a cocky grin.

She dug her hands on her hips. "We agreed we'd do most of this through emails."

"No, you suggested it. I never agreed."

"I sent you plenty of things you could have selected for me to get started. Now we're behind several days, and I can't get the painters here for another two days, all because you're playing games."

Jack dropped his feet, rose, and leaned a hip on the edge of the table. "I'm not playing games. You're my decorator—I need you here, in my office, to *decorate*."

A flare of annoyance crossed her face. "You're being ridiculous."

"I'm not the one who can't face me after what happened here the other day." He pointed to the chair.

Lauren's gaze darted to the chair. She blushed deep red and reached for her locket. Jack wondered what her attachment with it was.

Pulling out a folder from her briefcase, she opened it up on the table. "I'm here now."

If she didn't want to talk about it, fine. She could try to pretend nothing happened if it made her happy, but he was going to remind her that it did.

As he stepped closer, the scent of flowers and sunshine filled his senses. Damn, she made his mouth water. "So, what have you got to show me?"

He leaned over her shoulder, brushing slightly against her back. Sucking in a breath, she took a small step back, but not before he felt a tremble rake through her body. A smirk of satisfaction played on his lips.

"I'm thinking of keeping the walls neutral, that way your sporting memorabilia will be the main focus." Her voice shook slightly, and he knew she was trying hard to not act affected by their closeness.

He took a step closer. This time Lauren drew in a deep breath and stood her ground. Her false bravado didn't fool him.

"As for furniture, I'm hoping you're not into the stainless steel and glass look. I think it would feel too sterile and clinical." She flicked through a couple of pages, and once she found the one she was searching for, she tapped it with her finger. "See how the timbers and warm color fabrics are more inviting?"

"I thought we were going with a pink and purple color scheme?"

A cute huffing sound whispered past her lips. "I really should do it. It would serve you right. Do you like the pictures I've shown you?"

He hadn't looked at the folder since she opened it. Instead, he had been paying special attention to the curve of her neck. He wanted to trail his tongue along the smooth skin but answered, "It looks good." And he wasn't talking about the new color scheme.

She turned her head to look at him over her shoulder, probably noticing the husky tone in his voice. Her eyes widened as he closed the gap even more and pressed against her back, their faces only inches apart.

"Lauren, you're driving me insane." He trailed a finger down the smooth skin of her neck. A shiver shook her body. "I want to put my mouth on you, and I want you to want me to."

Her gaze flicked to his mouth, and her tongue darted out to lick her bottom lip. It was all the invitation he needed. Groaning, he turned her to him, cupped her face in his hands, and covered her lips with his own. Slow and sweet.

For a moment he thought she might stop him, and he prayed she wouldn't. As if answering his prayers, she gripped his shoulders and pulled him closer. He told himself to take it slow this time, but damn if he had any self-control. The kiss turned deep and urgent.

God, he wanted to lay her down on the floor and taste every inch of her. But he wouldn't. Not with Lauren. She wasn't a quick screw—even if her encouraging moan told him otherwise— and he wanted a lot more time with her. But that didn't mean he'd stop kissing her senseless.

Jack heard the muffled buzzing of a phone coming from inside Lauren's bag. He ignored it, and she did too, either that or she was too wrapped up in the kiss to notice it. The ringing stopped and Jack got back to focusing one-hundred percent on Lauren. Threading his fingers into her hair, the soft, silky strands tumbled into his hands. With unsteady hands, he gently brushed the hair away from her neck and placed his lips on her rapidly beating pulse.

The phone rang again. Unable to ignore it for the second time—it could be something important—he groaned at the interruption and pulled away. Lauren blinked up at him, and heat coiled low in his belly at the lust shining from her eyes. Red, swollen lips called to him, and he had to stop himself from taking them again.

"Your phone's ringing." His voice came out husky and raw.

"My phone?" She looked as dazed as Jack felt.

He nodded toward the bag hung over her shoulder.

Shaking her head as if reality finally sank in, she stepped away from him and fumbled in the bag, searching for her phone. "Hello?" she answered with a shaky voice. "Hi, Jaime." She paused, listening to the caller, then flicked out her wrist to look at her watch. "I can be there in about fifteen minutes." She disconnected the call and turned to Jack. "Something's come up at work, I need to go."

The need to keep touching her was strong, so he

shoved his hands into his pockets. "Go ahead with your suggestions. They sound good to me."

She nodded, said a quick goodbye, and left the office, avoiding eye contact.

Turning, he found Lauren's briefcase still sitting on the desk. Picking it up, he ran out after her, catching up with her just outside the building. "Lauren," he called out, and she stopped and turned around. He lifted up her briefcase. "Forget something?"

She smiled. "Thanks. I would have had to come back for it."

"I would've loved another visit." He grinned.

Red flushed her cheeks.

The breeze had blown a strand of hair onto her lips and he plucked it off and tucked it behind her ear. He couldn't help but lean in and plant a soft kiss on her mouth before walking back into his office.

Claire sipped iced tea as she sat at the same table in Mandy's Coffee House—giving her the same view of Jack's office—as the day she'd destroyed it. But instead of satisfaction for what she did to the office keeping her company, fury sat by her side.

Every day since her act of destruction Claire had sat at Mandy's at different times, watching the comings and goings from his office. She'd seen the cleanup crew arrive and remove the broken furniture, courtesy of her handiwork, and had laughed at Ellen looking scared every time the woman unlocked the building for work. Claire wanted to give Jack some time to think about what he'd done, so that when they reunited he would have missed her so much he'd give her anything she wanted.

A blonde woman sashaying her way to the building caught Claire's attention. Her grip tightened on the glass as she saw the blonde slut give her hair a quick tidy before pushing through the doors, no doubt wanting and willing to fill Claire's position. Claire's mouth twisted in a cruel sneer. She wasn't fooled by the briefcase the blonde held. The only position the bitch would be filling would be Jack's new office whore.

When the blonde slut walked out twenty minutes later, her hair looking tousled— which Claire was sure was from Jack's fingers—it was like a slap to the face. The fury that had consumed her now clenched at her chest and rammed a fist down her throat. It hadn't taken him long to find her replacement. And then when he ran after the whore like a horny dog, blood as hot as fire traveled through her veins. *How could he move on?* Jack belonged to her! But now some cheap blonde, who had no business fucking him, thought she could waltz right in and take him.

Not going to happen.

When Jack walked back into his office, Claire jumped up from the seat and raced out of the coffee shop, determined not to let the bitch out of her sight. She kept a few meters behind and watched as she got into a car. Thankfully, Claire's rented Mazda wasn't too far away. She hurried to the vehicle, got in, and pulled out onto the street, making sure she didn't get lost in the traffic.

Luck was on her side and she tailed the blonde until she stopped in a carpark behind a brick, cottage-style building and walked inside the shop. Claire pulled into a parking spot on the opposite side of the street, giving her a view of the shopfront.

Finally, after sweltering in the heat of the car for over an hour as she watched the woman move around the shop, the bitch left from the back entrance and got in her car, pulling out onto the street and driving away.

Claire tried to follow her again but lost sight of her in the heavy morning traffic.

There was no doubt in Claire's mind that the blonde was doing more than Jack's filing.

This bitch needed to be put down.

auren heard her phone ring as she stepped out of the shower. Grabbing the fluffy towel from the rail, she wrapped it around her and hurried into her bedroom. She picked the phone up from the bedside table and checked the caller ID. Her traitorous heart accelerated at full speed when she saw the name that lit up the small screen. Taking a deep breath, she answered.

Jack's unmistakable, sexy voice rumbled through the phone. "Hi, Lauren. Have I caught you at a bad time?"

As if he could somehow see her through the phone, she wrapped the towel tighter. "Hi, Jack. No, I was just…" She looked down at her bare, wet legs. It felt too intimate to tell him she'd just stepped out of the shower. "…cleaning the bathroom." With a shake of her head, she rolled her eyes. *Cleaning the bathroom?* "What can I do for you?"

"I need to talk to you about tomorrow."

"I left a message this afternoon with Ellen to let you know

that the painters would be there at seven. Is there a problem?" she asked while padding over to her underwear drawer.

"Yes, there's a problem. Why didn't you call me and give me the message yourself?"

Pulling the drawer open, she picked up a pair of undies and paused. "Because you were in a meeting and I told Ellen not to disturb you."

"You're not trying to avoid me again, are you? You have to come to terms with the fact that we are drawn to each other and what happened in my office, and every time we're together, will happen again. Now, you can try to deny it, but it's the truth. The quicker you realize that, the happier we'll both be."

Knees wobbly, she dropped down onto the side of the bed. "Jack, I'm not going to deny there's an attraction. But we have to keep things purely professional."

"It's too late for that. We passed being professional the first time we kissed." At the sound of the huskiness in his voice lust rippled along her spine and heated all her good parts.

Lauren glanced down at the underwear she held in her lap and threw the black, lacy panties toward the open drawer like they were a hot piece of coal. If she held onto underwear like that while Jack spoke in his sexy voice, she'd be tempted to let him see her wearing them.

She rose from the bed to look for something more appropriate. Finding a pair of white, nothingsexy-about-them cotton undies, she slid them on.

Maybe they had passed a point of no return, but that

didn't mean they needed to keep following a path which would lead nowhere. She needed to shut this conversation down before it went any further.

"Jack, I have to go. I just got out of the shower, and I'm wet…" She slapped her forehead.

"I thought you said you were cleaning the bathroom?" Jack didn't miss a beat.

"Umm…" Unable to think of a response quick enough, she said, "Bye, Jack."

"No! No, wait!" he yelled, stopping her from hanging up. "You can't tell me you're naked and then hang up." His voice sounded strained.

"I'm not naked, and I *am* hanging up now."

"Wait!" he stopped her again. "What *are* you wearing?" She heard eagerness in his voice.

The slutty devil on her left shoulder, because surely it couldn't be the innocent angel on her right one, answered, "I'm wearing nothing but black, lacy panties." Jack groaned just before she hit the *end call* button.

She flopped onto the bed and covered her burning face with her hands. So much for shutting things down before they went too far.

Kicking off his leather shoes, Jack stripped out of his suit and threw it on the bed. So, Lauren could be a sexy flirt when she wanted. He needed a long, cold shower after picturing her wearing nothing but black, lacy panties. The thought of Lauren in black, lacy anything was enough to get him rock-hard.

There were many women he could call—women who would be willing to solve his problem, with no strings attached—but he couldn't bring himself to call any of them. Lauren's image was burned into his brain, and until he had her where he wanted, he knew he wouldn't be satisfied with anyone else.

Going into the bathroom, Jack turned the water to full blast and stepped under the cold spray. The water only reduced his body's inferno temperature to a simmer. Picking up the soap, he lathered his body.

There had been no reason for him to call Lauren tonight. Calling her about the message was just an excuse. In truth, he'd been thinking about her, something he'd been doing a lot lately, and before he knew it, he'd dialed her number. Her sexy voice had turned him on instantly.

Turning the water off, he dried himself and padded naked into his bedroom. The shower hadn't done much to fix his rock-hard problem. Pulling the covers back from the bed, he slipped naked between the cool cotton sheets, and stared up at the ceiling.

Never had a woman invaded his mind the way Lauren did. Not even Amy—the only *real* relationship he'd ever had. Real, because it had lasted a record five months. He'd liked Amy, even tried convincing himself he loved her, but they fought more often than they were happy. Every time he'd gone away for footy she'd accused him of sleeping with the groupies that hung around their hotel. She never trusted him, and if he were honest, it would have only been a matter of time before temptation had gotten the better of him. So he decided to let her go before he broke her heart even more.

And now Lauren had him wanting to put his hands on her and *only* her. Being with anyone else was not an option. A hundred naked groupies offering up all kinds of kinky services would not have gotten him as aroused as the sound of Lauren's sweet-as-honey voice. He rubbed a hand down his face. How the hell did that happen?

Not only was she drop-dead gorgeous, she was funny and smart too. She fascinated him.

He wanted to have her in every way possible, but he also wanted to get to know more about her.

Lauren wanted to try to fight the attraction and wanted to convince herself Jack was everything bad she wanted to stay away from, but he knew she was fighting a losing battle. If she thought this wasn't going anywhere further, she was delusional. She needed to get this *Mr. Pretty* problem out of her head, which he was happy to help her do, and explore her options—him. His gut tightened at the thought of her exploring her options with any other man. A reaction he was not familiar with.

Chapter 17

*D*uring the next few days Jack's office was a whirlwind of activity. Lauren was constantly checking on painters, electricians, and furniture deliveries. It pleased her to see the office looking like a place of business.

With all the activity going on, they hadn't had any time alone. She didn't know whether to be happy or disappointed. She decided to choose happy, but deep down she didn't really believe it.

Even though they were never alone, Jack's hooded, sexy eyes followed her, making no secret about watching her. Excitement flowed in all the right places. She had to work really hard to ignore his sex-me-up eyes or she'd be tempted to take him up on what they offered and never get any work done.

But he was *s-o-o-o* pretty. No, pretty wasn't a good enough word for him. He went beyond pretty. Masculinity oozed from his every pore. His body, built for power, filled out his dress pants and steel-gray shirt in a way that should be illegal. Twice that morning, she'd been caught staring at him. Although he was kind enough not to say anything in front of the workers, his cocky grin and mischievous eyes twinkled with understanding.

Lauren was getting to the point where if she didn't get her hands on him, she'd combust like a cheap, bargain-basement heater. And then where would she be? Her *no Mr. Pretty* rules would be broken and she'd ultimately be left alone and heartbroken once again. *Heartbroken? Where did that come from?* Alone...maybe. Heartbroken...definitely not. That would mean investing her heart in him, and she knew that would be a big mistake.

When Stacey, the courier, staggered into the office carrying packages of framed football jerseys Jack raced over to take them out of her hands. Stacey, with her short denim shorts, tight pink tank top, and mane of long, black gorgeous hair, smiled her thanks and gave him a comeback-to-my-place-so-I-can-handle-your-package look. Jack smiled back, all sexy and flirty. Lauren's chest tightened and heat threatened to steam from her ears. God, she could kick her own ass for falling for those bedroom eyes.

Hearing Stacey giggle—*giggle!*—at something Jack said had her thinking of castration and how messy it would get.

Marching over to them, Lauren snatched the electronic scanner thingy from Stacey's hand and scribbled her signature on the screen. She thanked Stacey with sugar-sweet politeness and sent her on her merry way.

Jack's low chuckle behind her had her body responding like it usually did—turned on and slutty. Damn her traitorous body.

"Careful, if I didn't know better, I'd say you look jealous."

Lauren knew the truth of what he said would be flashing in her eyes, so she turned her attention to the delivery. Ignoring his comment, she busied herself tearing off the protective packaging from the jerseys Stacey had delivered.

"You threw Stacey out because she was flirting with me." Obviously, he wasn't going to let it go.

She made an unladylike snort. "Why should I care if you two were flirting?" She stepped back to inspect the frames.

"*I* was being friendly."

"Again, don't care. Flirt with whoever you want."

Carrying one of the frames over to the wall she wanted to hang it on, she carefully leaned it against the fresh paint. She turned to get the next one but Jack stood as solid as a brick wall in her way, looking like he was enjoying himself a little too much. When she tried to step around the conceited jerk, two strong hands dropped on her shoulders, stopping her getaway.

She glanced over at Ron, the electrician, who was on his knees screwing in the new power outlets. White earbuds stuck out from his ears and he was singing out of tune to what sounded like an AC/DC song.

"I think you do care." Jack's emerald eyes flashed heat.

"Well, I don't," she replied, trying hard not to let his

gaze turn her into mush. There was a very good reason she wanted to stay away from Jack, and the incident with Stacey had reminded her why.

"Your tone suggests otherwise." The corners of his lips turned up into a smile, and she wanted to slap it off his face for being an over-confident, cocky jerk.

"You're reading too much into it. Stacey was acting very unprofessional. This is a place of business, not a pick-up bar. She's here to do a job, not waste my time." She resisted the urge to add *and she wanted to do you!* because that would've really made her sound jealous.

Shrugging her shoulders, she tried to shake him off with no luck. "I'm here to do a job, so flirt with whoever you want on your own time."

"I'm going to tell you again, I wasn't *flirting* with her."

Lauren suppressed a sigh of frustration. "Look, Jack. I know you probably can't help it, it's in the Mr. Pretty's nature—"

His firm grip tightened on her shoulders. "We're not back to this *Mr. Pretty* bullshit again, are we? Because if you tell me I'm a *Mr. Pretty* one more time, I'll be extremely pissed."

She averted her eyes. It was exactly what she'd been going to say. Jack probably couldn't help but flirt with every attractive woman who entered the room. Well, to be fair, apart from Ellen and herself, Stacey had been the only other woman to come into the office. But the number didn't matter; it was still in a Mr. Pretty's nature.

He cupped her face with his large, strong hands, traced the pad of his thumb along her bottom lip, and with hooded eyes, he asked, "Do I need to kiss some sense into you?"

Yes, please, she wanted to yell and be damned with anything she believed in, but instead, she shook her head.

His head lowered, his lips hovering above hers. "I'm not a *Mr. Pretty*, and the sooner you see that, the better. I may smile at pretty women, but that doesn't mean I want to sleep with them. I've left that position open for you."

The words and the deep voice they were spoken in knocked the breath out of her.

"Morning!" a cheerful voice called into the room.

Dropping his forehead for a beat onto Lauren's, Jack cursed before letting her go. Using the distraction of the visitor, Lauren put distance between them and sucked air back into her oxygen-starved lungs.

Leah walked into the office, pushing a pram in front of her, looking well-rested and happy compared to the last time Lauren had seen her. Upon spotting Lauren, she paused, then her gaze darted down at the pram. When she looked at Lauren again her eyes looked suspiciously moist. Jack must have told her about Abby.

Leah turned to leave. "Sorry. I see you're busy, Jack, so I'll come back later. It's nice to see you again, Lauren."

"No, don't go." Lauren stopped her.

Leah again glanced inside the pram, looking unsure.

Lauren needed to convince her she didn't always act like a raving lunatic. So, on shaky legs, she made her way over to the pram. She stopped a couple of feet away from the baby but still couldn't bring herself to look inside. "Is

Emma feeling better?" The question came out through stiff lips.

Lauren felt Jack move up behind her, his warm presence a comforting support, and she couldn't help but lean back against him.

"Yes, much better, thanks. She had an ear infection, and after a course of antibiotics she's back to normal." Leah looked at Jack with wary eyes.

A gurgling sound and squeal came from inside the pram, grabbing Lauren's attention. She sucked up the courage to look down and saw two blue, shiny eyes staring up at her. A tight pressure squeezed at her heart, but the pain that normally hit every time she saw a baby didn't hit quite so hard; only a dull ache thumped at her chest. Unable to stop staring at the precious baby, a smile —a real smile, not some semblance of one—spread across Lauren's face.

Reaching a trembling hand inside the pram, she touched Emma's velvety soft cheek, and the baby gurgled happily, making Lauren laugh. "You're so precious, aren't you, beautiful girl?" she whispered.

For the first time since losing Abby, it didn't feel like her heart had been ripped out of her chest and torn into tiny pieces. She wasn't sure what the change was. Maybe it was having the solid presence of Jack standing behind her, silently offering support.

Glancing back up at Leah, she saw her blinking away tears, but pretended not to notice.

"I'm so glad she's feeling better."

She turned to Jack and was taken aback by the

concern etched on his face. The concern appeared genuine, like he actually cared. She knew if she turned into a blubbering heap again, he'd be there offering comfort. He brushed his hand across her cheek. She leaned into his palm and closed her eyes for a moment, soaking up the affection and concern.

"Are you okay?" he asked.

She thought about his question for a moment, then answered, "Yes." And for the first time since the horrible day she lost her precious Abby, she really meant it.

Chapter 18

When Lauren left to go back to her shop, Jack and Leah, with Emma in tow of course, made their way across the street to grab a coffee. After making their purchase, they strolled along the foot-path, past the cafés, and headed toward Lang Park.

Although it was only nine-thirty in the morning, it was already hot. The sky was clear of clouds, and the sun's rays heated through Jack's shirt. They passed the swings, where a group of small children played, their mothers watching over them protectively.

Sitting on an empty park bench underneath a Jacaranda tree, they sipped their coffee and watched Emma blink heavily, her eyes finally falling shut.

Leah was the first to speak. "I love what Lauren's done to the office. I know it's not finished, but it's going to look amazing."

Stretching out his legs, Jack balanced the take-away coffee on his thigh. "I agree. She has great taste."

"She sure does," she said, then nudged Jack in the ribs with her elbow, "with men too."

Jack raised an eyebrow.

"She is totally into you." When Jack made a noncommittal noise in his throat, she continued. "She is…big time. The way you two looked at each other in the office made sparks fly like fireworks." She patted his knee. "I'm so happy you've finally woken up to yourself and stopped dating the…well, let's just say, women who don't deserve you."

Leah made no secret she didn't like the women he dated. She wanted him to find the right one and settle down. It was frustrating that Leah and his mother were of the same mind. But he'd never been interested in finding someone who made him want to give up the lifestyle he enjoyed.

"I don't do the dating thing."

"No, you only have sex with them. When was the last time you went out with a woman because you were interested in *her* and not what the sheets on her bed look like?"

"I never look at the sheets." He grinned.

She nudged him in the ribs again, this time harder.

Jack sighed. "Not including Lauren? Not since Amy."

Pulling a bright pink muslin wrap out of the baby bag at her feet, Leah covered the pram

with it. Jack assumed it was to stop the sun from shining on Emma. "You went out on a date with Lauren?"

Jack pinched the bridge of his nose then undid the top two buttons of his shirt. It was either getting hotter or the conversation was making him uncomfortable. "Well, it wasn't technically a date. I asked Lauren to meet me for a drink to discuss work. I used work as an excuse to get her to meet me." Man, that sounded lame. Never had he used trickery to get a woman to go out with him. He was losing his touch.

"You tricked her?" Leah's eyebrows disappeared into her hairline before she tipped her head back and laughed. "Oh, this is too much. My big, handsome brother had to trick a woman to go out with him. Wait until I tell James, he's going to have kittens! Why didn't you just ask her out?" she asked, still laughing.

He rubbed his sweaty palms along the tops of his thighs. "I did, she said no."

Leah wiped away the tears that had sprung from her eyes and said, "Let me get this right. Out of all the women you could've called, who would've been more than happy to meet up with you, you picked a woman you needed to trick to meet you?"

"Leah, drop it." Her reaction was becoming really annoying. If they were home, he would've wrestled the brat to the ground and sat on her until she stopped laughing. Childish games they still played from time to time.

Leah must have noticed Jack wasn't finding the conversation amusing and sobered up. She stared at him for a long time, like she was trying to work out what was going on inside his head. "You haven't been in the social pages with a new conquest in days, and I have to wonder if Lauren has something to do with that."

He knew Lauren had everything to do with it, and he still needed to work out what it all meant. This wasn't how he rolled. He worked hard, played harder, and enjoyed the company of beautiful women. But it was Lauren, who fought hard to stay away from him, who filled him with more excitement than all the women he had ever been with.

"I like Lauren. I think she's great." *More than great*, he thought. "But if you think it's going to lead to anything serious, you're wrong." He'd like it to lead into his bedroom, or hers, but deep down, if he was honest, he couldn't see Lauren being the type of woman he could have fun with for the night with no strings attached.

Leah shook her coffee cup and frowned, probably because it was empty, then placed it on the seat. "We'll see." She looked skeptical. "But can I tell you something?"

"Will you keep it to yourself if I say no?"

She stuck her tongue out, and he chuckled. It would be a miracle if she kept things to herself. If she had something to say, she'd say it whether he wanted to hear it or not. "Lauren isn't a woman you can mess around with. She's not a two-in-the-morning booty call you can forget the moment the deed is done."

He'd already figured that out, but he said, "You've been spending too much time with Mum, you're starting to sound just like her."

Leah laughed. "Mum calls your women booty calls?"

"Not exactly, but she knows Lauren isn't like them."

"I like Lauren. I think she could be good for you. But if you're not feeling the same way she is about you, then leave her alone."

Jack scrubbed his face with his hands. He really didn't

want to be talking to Leah about his love life, or lack of one. "You don't have to worry about Lauren. She's made it perfectly clear she wants nothing to do with me."

"Huh," Leah said on a puff of breath. "From what I saw, it looks like she wants *everything* to do with you."

"Are you reading those Mills and Boon romance books again? Because I think you've got love hearts over your eyes."

"I'm being serious. I know what I saw—and that's a woman who wants more than your body."

"This time, sis, you are totally wrong. Apparently I fall into the category of a Mr. Pretty."

"A what?"

"Mr. Pretty. Rich, successful, and good-looking," he said, holding up a finger as he named each item on the list.

"And that's a bad thing?"

He'd wondered the same thing when he first learned what met the requirements.

Jack previously told Leah about Lauren losing a baby and now he gave her a watered-down version about Graham Stone and what Lauren had gone through.

"Oh, that poor woman. How much heartbreak can one person take?" She brushed a tear from her cheek. "She's probably right, you should stay away."

What the hell? Swiveling his head, Jack stared at her with surprise. "I'm nothing like Graham. A minute ago you told me she'd be good for me!" he said, taking offense.

She placed a hand on his arm. "Jack, I have no doubt

that you would never leave a woman pregnant and alone. But your track record isn't great. If you're not serious about Lauren, leave her alone. I'd hate for her to have to go through heartbreak again." When he tried to speak she held out a hand to stop him. "There may be sparks flying around you two, but I can understand why she wouldn't want to take the risk with you." He tried to speak only to be stopped again.

"You grew up in the footy community where relationships, let's face it, weren't the best. Then you have women throwing themselves at you because of your money and fame. Your good looks were the icing on the cake, and you knew exactly how to use your pretty-boy looks to lure them in. I have to admit, apart from Amy, you did only go for the women who never expected happily ever after. And Lauren will want happily ever after."

Tension pinched the back of his neck. "You don't even know her."

"I know her type, and she's not someone you can fool around with. You either take this seriously or you leave her alone."

Leah's words rang with truth, and it wasn't anything he hadn't already been thinking. No, he wasn't like the asshole Graham Stone, but had he treated women any better? Most of the time he could pick the good-time girls and no one got hurt. Then along came Amy. She wasn't a booty call. He knew she wanted the ring on her finger and the happily ever after, and he had tried to believe he could do the relationship thing. It didn't work, and Amy ended up getting hurt.

He never wanted to hurt Lauren, and if things were to go any further, that's exactly what might happen. Maybe Leah, for once in her life, was right. He should leave Lauren alone. But why did stepping away feel so damn hard to do?

Chapter 19

*L*auren checked her watch for the third time. Belinda was twenty minutes late.

By now Lauren should know that Belinda never turned up on time. The woman got a cheap thrill out of making Lauren wait. If she was so desperate for money, the least she could do was show up on time, and yet Lauren was the one who always sat around waiting for her. Lauren would give her another ten minutes, and then what…leave? No, she couldn't, not unless she wanted Belinda running to Graham.

After all these years, Lauren still cared about keeping the secret, even though she'd grown past being ashamed of having an affair with a married man. She'd finally realized Graham had taken advantage of a young girl starving for affection. Lauren came from a home with no love and he used it to manipulate her. The experience had changed her life, and she was the person she was today because of it—

strong, independent, and ready to face what the world threw at her.

Well, all except for love. Her experience still had her believing love was a fairy tale. But now life had thrown Jack at her; a temptation of the highest degree. Whenever he glanced her way her heart skidded to a stop and her brain turned to mush. The *Mr. Pretty* radar shut down as soon as he entered the room and she was left to fend for herself, and she'd been doing a poor job of it.

The nineteen-year-old, battle-scarred girl still trapped inside her screamed *you'll get your feelings crushed. Back away now and no one will get hurt!* But the hot-blooded woman wanting to break free interrupted, *who said anything about feelings? Have fun!*

Lauren knew she couldn't keep her body on ice forever. But could she really take Ava and Jade's advice and only have fun with Jack? If she kept her heart detached and they both knew where they stood, then no one would get hurt, right?

This was why she was better off alone. Relationships, or even flings, were too complicated.

Once again, she checked her watch. Still no Belinda, and she didn't have time to wait around much longer. A delivery had arrived at Jack's office and she told him she'd come by soon to go through the boxes. A delivery dropped off by Stacey, who'd been doing a lot of them lately. Lauren had no doubt that Stacey had purposely kept boxes back so she could make extra trips. The woman still flirted with Jack, but he'd only smile and thank her for the delivery. Deep down it pleased Lauren to watch Stacey try to turn up the heat with Jack only to walk away empty-handed.

Lauren had chosen to meet Belinda at Mandy's, a coffee shop across the street from Jack's office, so she could run straight over after this unpleasant meeting.

The last of the deliveries had arrived, and her time with Jack was coming to an end. Once the final lot of boxes were unpacked and the items sorted through, her job was complete. That meant she had no reason to see him anymore. And she wouldn't have to worry about trying to control herself around him; didn't have to worry about whether she was going to take her friends' advice and let go and get naked with him, because he wouldn't be in her life anymore.

That should have made her happy. She could move on with her life and not have to deal with the turmoil that coursed through her body and mind every time Jack was near. So why did her belly sink and her throat tighten at the thought of never seeing him again? Clearing her throat, she took a sip of the cooling latté and tried to pretend she didn't care so much.

But she couldn't resist glancing out the coffee shop window toward Jack's office. The sun reflected off the office windows, making visibility inside impossible. Lauren's days turning up to work at Jack's had always gotten her excited. And to be honest, it wasn't the job that made her heart race when she got there, it was Jack. But all things must come to an end, and the sooner it did, the better off she'd be. Like ripping off a Band-Aid, it would only hurt for a second, and then she could get back to her normal *Mr. Pretty* free life, free of complications. He'd been nothing more than a job, so she'd have to let her Mr. Pretty go. She shook her head. It was a somber thought; he wasn't *her Mr. Pretty*, and never would be.

Lauren was lost in thought when Belinda finally arrived. She blew into the café on a cloud of cigarette smoke and cheap perfume. Belinda pulled out the chair opposite Lauren, and the timber chair creaked as she sat down hard. Clicking her fingers at a nearby waitress, she demanded coffee.

Belinda was dressed in a pair of faded black frayed shorts that looked two sizes too small and did nothing to hide her chunky legs. The purple t-shirt she'd squeezed into, that read *I'm your princess*, strained to cover her flabby middle. Her dirty blonde hair hung in a limp mess at her shoulders. Lines cracked the sides of her mouth, and red blemishes marked her puffy skin.

Years of smoking and drinking hadn't been kind, and she looked a lot more than two years older than Lauren.

"So have ya got the money?" Belinda never bothered pretending to be nice.

"I have most of it."

Jack had insisted he pay Lauren the whole amount up-front, but Lauren refused, even though she could have used it to pay off Belinda sooner. She'd never charged a client the full amount until they were completely satisfied with the end results. He wasn't happy with the arrangement, but reluctantly agreed.

Fidgeting with an orange lighter in her hand, Belinda flicked the flame on and off like she was dying to light up another cigarette. The stale smoke clinging to her smelled like she'd already smoked a couple of packs. "I told you I need all of it."

The waitress arrived and placed Belinda's coffee on the table.

Belinda took a sip, then frowned. "This tastes like shit." She tore open three sugar packets and poured them into the cup.

"You've asked for a lot of money. I'll have the rest at the end of the week." Lauren pulled out an envelope from her purse and slid it across the table. Belinda could take it or leave it.

Looking eager to get her hands on the money, Belinda snatched the envelope up, ripped it open, and counted the cash. When she appeared satisfied that she had most of it, she put the envelope in a grungy-looking bag.

"You better have the rest by the end of the week." She coughed a smoker's mucous cough. "Or I'd have to ask Graham for the rest." Then she laughed, if you could call the hacking sound she made laughing. "Ya know it might be fun spillin' your dirty little secret just for the laughs."

Anger rolled deep in Lauren's gut, and she stiffened. "We agreed I'd give you money when you needed it."

"Relax, I'm kiddin'," she sniggered. "Geez, you're so touchy."

It would be so much easier for Lauren to tell Belinda to go to hell and let her go to whoever she wanted with the twisted story. It would finally get her sister off her back and out of her life, and she'd never have to deal with her again. But she didn't want to ruin people's lives. Not because Graham deserved her discretion, but because he had an innocent wife and young daughter who would be thrown into a media frenzy. They were the perfect family with a glamorous life. Australia's much loved family would be brought down in an instant.

The attention Lauren would receive would get ugly too. Even though she'd been a naïve teenager who didn't know she was having an affair with a married man, she'd be portrayed as the home-wrecking whore who seduced a happily married man and then tried trapping him by getting pregnant. The media loved a good scandal, and they'd play it up as big as they could get it. That kind of attention would ruin her reputation and probably her business. This had to stay quiet, so she had no other choice but to keep paying off Belinda.

"How's Mum doing?" Lauren asked out of curiosity.

Belinda choked on the coffee and took a moment to clear her throat. "She died."

"She died? Why the hell didn't you tell me?"

Belinda shrugged. "Didn't think you'd care." She took a gulp of her coffee.

Did she care? A cold emptiness took over her heart. It was hard to care with so much built-up resentment.

"When is the funeral?"

Belinda used the back of her hand to wipe the dribble of coffee from her chin. "Last week. Sorry, did you want to go?" she asked with mock sweetness.

No, she wouldn't have gone, but she didn't like having the choice taken away from her.

"You still could've called."

Placing a hand on her chest, her fingers stained yellow from smoking, Belinda said with sarcasm, "Aww, I didn't know you cared. Anyway, if you're interested, she had another stroke that finished her off."

Lauren kept her clenched fists in her lap or she'd be tempted to wipe the smugness from

Belinda's face. "How did you pay for the funeral?"

"I made an arrangement with a guy who works in the gardens at the funeral home. He asked his boss for a payment plan for me," she said, winking.

Lauren shuddered. She didn't want to think about the kind of *arrangement* she'd made.

"You still could've told me what was happening." She kept her voice smooth and in control even though fury boiled like hot lava in her veins.

Belinda narrowed her red-rimmed eyes at Lauren. "You didn't give a shit about Mum, so why would I tell you? You didn't miss much. No one turned up 'cept for me. The priest said a few words and it was done. It was very moving." She wiped a pretend tear from her eye. "Well, my dear sister, as much as I've enjoyed our little chat, I must be off." Tossing her head back, Belinda swallowed the remaining coffee, then banged the cup down onto the table. She waved her fingers and said, "See ya soon." And she left as she'd entered—in a cloud of cigarette smoke and cheap perfume.

Chapter 20

Sitting motionless, Lauren stared at the cars and people walking past the coffee shop. Her mother had died, the funeral already held, and she hadn't been there for either. If Belinda didn't need money, she wondered if she would have been told at all. She doubted it.

It shouldn't matter, because she'd made it a point a long time ago to stay away from that side of her life. The woman who was supposed to be a mother to her never really was and Belinda always hated Lauren's very existence. If it wasn't for the money Belinda demanded, Lauren would never see her.

Would she have gone to the funeral so she could say goodbye? No, she had said her goodbyes when she left the house as a young and scared teenager. Now that Dorothy was dead, should she forgive her for such a shitty childhood? Even after all these years she couldn't bring herself to forgive the woman. The memory of Dorothy's icy, unfeeling eyes would burn forever in her mind.

It didn't matter now. There would be no goodbyes, chances of forgiveness, or telling Dorothy to go to hell as they lowered her casket in the ground.

Hot tears burned behind her eyes. Not tears of sadness, but tears of anger. She thought she'd stopped being angry a long time ago. Thought she had even accepted her past and all the ghosts within it. So feeling the old emotions rage and open up like old wounds surprised her.

Vision blurry, she pulled out what looked like a twenty-dollar note and placed it on the table. With her head down she rushed out of the coffee shop and ran smack into a firm, solid, warm wall.

"I'm sorry." Lauren tried stepping around the wall, but two familiar, strong hands gripped her arms.

"Lauren, what's wrong?" Concern sounded in Jack's voice, but she didn't dare look at him because he might witness another meltdown.

"I'm in a hurry, Jack. I'm sorry, but I don't have time for our meeting." Her voice shook.

"Fuck the meeting. Lauren, look at me."

Humiliation held tight and she shook her head.

Placing a finger under her chin and tilting it up, he mumbled a curse under his breath as

he examined her face. "What happened?" he demanded.

"Nothing, Jack. Please, I have to go." She tried to break free from his grip with no success.

"I'm not letting you go anywhere like this." The firm tone left no room for argument.

"Jack, I'm fine." She tried to smile in the hopes he'd see she was okay and let her go. She couldn't let him see her in such a state again. Actually, maybe if she told him how messed up her life was he'd leave her well and truly alone. Wasn't that what she wanted? Her brain and her heart were in a tug-of-war.

"Let's go." Holding her hand, he led her across the road and toward his car.

She pulled him to a stop, and he turned to look at her. "My car's back the other way."

"I know." He continued to pull her along only for her to stop him again.

"I want to go to my car."

"You're in no condition to drive."

Normally she would have dug in her heels, but she didn't have the energy to argue over this, so she let him pull her behind him.

When they reached his car, he opened the passenger door and she slid onto soft leather seats warmed by the summer heat. Jack slid into the driver's side, started the ignition, and flicked the air conditioning to high. She was thankful for the sudden blast of cold air that cooled her flushed face. She could only imagine how red and blotchy it must look.

Driving along Carter Street, Jack turned onto Hamilton Avenue without saying a word. Grateful for the silence, Lauren glanced out the passenger side window. Retail shops along the strip had closed for the day, but the restaurants were getting ready for Friday night trade. The silence grew thick; she needed to say something. "I don't normally cry so much." Jack glanced at her then back at the road.

"It's been a long time since I've cried, and unfortunately, you've witnessed it twice within a few weeks. Sorry about that." She tried to laugh but it sounded flat.

"Are you going to tell me what happened?" he asked, keeping his eyes on the road.

"Will you stop asking if I say no?"

"No."

Letting out a shaky laugh, she turned her attention to the passenger side window, not yet ready to talk. After ten minutes they entered a part of town known as the sporting hub. The area had been designed for football, soccer, and cricket fields. Bicycle tracks and footpaths led down to the beaches of Brimland Point.

"This isn't the way to my house." Why wasn't he taking her straight home?

"I know."

She turned to glare at him. "Are you going to tell me where you're taking me?"

"Are you going to tell me what happened when I found you?" Taking his eyes off the road for a beat, he glanced at her with a raised eyebrow.

It wasn't likely he would let the scene outside the coffee shop drop, but she wasn't ready to open up. "You're close with your family, I think that's great."

Lauren often wondered how different life would have turned out if she'd been born into a normal, loving family.

Would she have been so easily seduced by Graham? And if so, would her family have loved and supported her? Those were questions she would never know the answers to.

"They're a pain in my ass," he complained as he kept his eyes on the road, letting her change the subject.

Lauren chuckled and rested her head on the headrest. "But you love them." She stated the obvious. Often when Jack's mother, Susan, visited the shop she'd beam with pride and love when speaking about her children. She talked of family dinners, birthdays, and any celebration where she could gather them all together. Love like that was the greatest gift to give a child.

"They're okay," he grumbled, but there was a smile on his face.

"What made you decide on a football career? Henderson's Sports has been around for years, did your dad ever want you to follow that path instead of playing football?" Talking to Jack about his life was much better than thinking about her own.

"He would have liked it, but football was my passion. He knew I wouldn't be happy doing anything else until I gave footy my best shot. I trained my ass off until I got selected to play for the Stars."

She tilted her head toward him, studied his profile, and noticed, not for the first time, a small bump on the bridge of his nose. The only imperfection on his otherwise perfect face, but the small bump made him look even hotter.

"So you've been playing for the Stars your entire career? Did you ever want to play for another club?"

Checking his mirrors, he changed lanes and entered a quiet street. "Other clubs offered me ridiculous amounts of money to play for their teams, but I didn't play for the paycheck. It was about the game. Having a ball in my hand and doing whatever I could to get it over the line. The thrill is amazing. The Stars gave me my break, and they were always good to me. I had no reason to leave."

He was loyal and committed. Guilt niggled in her chest for always thinking the worst of him. The magazine articles Jade had shared with her never showed that side of him. At the thought of the articles Lauren remembered—because they weren't easy to forget and were now saved on her phone—the photos Jade had sent of Jack modeling for a Calvin Klein ad.

"So did you give up footy for a modeling career?"

Swinging his head toward her, Jack frowned. She bit her twitching lip to stop from laughing. Those photos were *not* a laughing matter. She'd lost count of the number of times she'd viewed them. They were the kind of photos that invoked dreams of the erotic kind.

"You saw the magazine shoot?" he said, deadpan.

"Jade mentioned you were the league's pretty boy, but I never thought you would give it up for modeling."

He made a disgruntled noise.

"What's the matter, Jack, are you not happy with how the photos turned out? Were your abs not chiseled enough, or your package didn't look…big enough?"

This time when Jack threw her a disgusted glare she burst out laughing.

Pulling to a stop, he leaned his arm behind Lauren's

seat and pinned her with his sexy green eyes. "You tell me, Lauren. You've sat on my lap...did the photos give it justice?" Lauren blinked and swallowed hard, unable to speak.

When his gaze dropped to her lips, heat stormed down south and she squirmed in the seat.

Was he going to kiss her? Did she want him to? Her girly parts screamed yes.

Waiting for an answer, he gave her a knowing, sexy grin before finally turning away. He stuck his hand out the window and punched a code into a security pad. A large, silver roller door rattled as it lifted in front of them.

With the sexed-up connection broken, she blew out the breath she'd been holding. Examining her surroundings, she didn't recognize the building they had stopped in front of. She leaned forward in her seat and looked out the windscreen and up toward the top of the building.

The sign above them read *Brimland Point Football Stadium. Home of the Flaming Stars.*

When the door opened fully, Jack drove slowly inside a dark, underground carpark.

Lauren peered into the dim, empty carpark and asked, "What are we doing here?"

"This is Friday night fun." He unbuckled the seatbelt, reached in the backseat for a black sports bag with the Flaming Stars logo on it, and grinned.

Lauren knew little about football, but she knew, courtesy of Jade, that the season hadn't started yet. Jade would have mentioned if there was a game on; she went to all the home games. "Is the footy on tonight?" she asked anyway.

"No." He unzipped the bag and rummaged around inside like he was checking to ensure he had everything, then zipped it shut again.

Jack's elusive answer had her blowing out a frustrated breath. "Are you going to tell me why we're here?"

"I'm training."

Training? Was he playing footy again? "Isn't your modeling career paying you enough?" A smirk played on her lips. If he wouldn't explain why the hell they were there, she could at least have some fun at his expense.

Jack glowered.

Lauren laughed.

"I train a few local kids two nights a month. I remembered I said I'd meet you and when I saw you at the coffee shop I was coming over to tell you we needed to reschedule." Meeting her gaze, he said, "I haven't forgotten the condition I found you in. You *will* tell me what happened."

"You could have taken me home," she said, still not ready to talk about her meeting with Belinda.

"And have you miss out on all the fun?" He grinned. "Friday night training is action packed. Where else would you want to be?"

After the meeting she should have had with Jack, her plans for the night had comprised of pajamas, popcorn, and a *Friends* marathon. Watching Jack train a bunch of kids sounded more exciting than her pathetic night home alone.

He opened the car door, slid out, and flung the bag over his shoulder. Lauren followed him. The carpark, despite the warm summer night, felt cool and damp. A closed-up, musty smell wafted in the air.

"Why do you train these kids? Is it part of some kind of contract you still have with the Stars?"

He stopped in front of dark red double doors and frowned at her. "There's no contract." "So why do you do it?" Why would Jack give up his time to train kids?

"I do it because I want to. I do it because I love doing it. I don't get paid."

Was this a publicity thing? Was it a way to help clean up his tarnished reputation? "If you don't get paid, what *do* you get out of it?"

He stared at her like she'd grown another head. "What I get out of it is I'm able to encourage these kids to get out on a footy field and do what they love. Encourage them to follow their dreams no matter who tells them they have no chance. I get to watch the excitement on a kid's face when he catches a ball for the first time after he's missed every other one. I get to watch a kid score a try when he's the slowest kid on the field." He shrugged. "That's why I do it."

Dammit. Lauren wanted to shrink into a tiny ball and roll into a crack in the concrete floor. She felt like the biggest fool for thinking Jack was only in it for some personal gain. He wasn't doing it for money or the exposure; he was training kids because he wanted them to have a chance at doing something they loved. Why did she keep getting things wrong with him? First she discovered he was loyal and committed, and now she added compassionate and kind to a long list of great qualities.

"Jack, I'm sorry…"

He shook his head. "Your opinion of me is low because of your *Mr. Pretty* theory. Maybe now you'll start to realize not all men fall into the same category." Where was that crack in the floor she needed to roll into?

Jack pointed over his shoulder at the double doors. "You wanna come in here and help me change into my training gear?" He lightened the mood with a sexy grin. And boy did it sounded tempting.

"I'll wait out here." She folded her arms across her chest and pretended she didn't want to run in there with him.

Jack chuckled. He pointed behind her at a long, narrow tunnel. "Head down there and it will take you straight through to the grandstand. I'll be out in a few minutes."

Jack set his bag down in an empty cubicle, stripped off his clothes, and put on his training gear.

The smell of Deep Heat—a pain relieving rub—and sweaty men filled the room. He took a deep breath of the pungent air. Memories of mateship, hours of hard work, sore muscles, and achievement always came flooding back when he entered the change rooms. God, he missed the game. If he hadn't busted his knee so bad he'd still be wearing the red and gold colors and leading the guys out onto the field.

But life throws curve balls now and then, and he couldn't complain about his changed career path. Taking over Henderson's, putting his own stamp on it, and growing it bigger than what it was had given him the same excitement as winning the NRL grand final.

His mind drifted back to Lauren. His stomach had dropped to the floor when she'd rushed out of the coffee shop like the hounds from hell were chasing her. The distressed look on her face and sad eyes made him wish he could make whatever her demons were all go away. She hadn't been ready to talk about it in the car. He'd give her a little time, but he was determined to find out what had happened. It wasn't good for her to lock up those feelings when they were causing such grief. A strong desire to help take that pain away hit hard.

What was it about Lauren that made him want to protect her from the world? He bent down to tie the laces up on his boots. He never wanted to be that kind of man for anyone before. But for Lauren he needed to be the man she could trust, rely on…deserve. Dammit, how could he prove it and make her believe he wasn't a typical Mr. Pretty?

Being with Lauren made him believe there really could be more to life than one-night stands and booty calls. Jack wanted to kiss away the pain and sadness projecting from her eyes, and give her everything she longed for.

He flicked the light switch, sending the change room

into darkness, and headed toward the field. He chuckled to himself. Who in their right mind would have thought Jack Henderson, womanizer and party boy, could be blindsided by a woman? Every part of him had been occupied by a sexy, sweet, loving, and caring woman, and he kinda liked it.

Chapter 21

*L*auren made her way through the cool, narrow tunnel until she came to the side of the football field. To the left and right of her rose a huge grandstand which could easily seat a few thousand people. Never having been to a live game before—no matter how many times Jade had tried to convince her to come along —and only seeing snippets of games on the TV, she was surprised by the enormity of the stadium.

A group of women sat at the grandstand to her left, so she made her way up a couple rows of stairs toward them. She sat next to a woman with brown, wavy hair and penciled-in eyebrows. She wore a Flaming Stars jersey, and when she leaned forward to place her coffee cup on the ground Lauren spotted the name *Henderson*, in big capital letters, over the number three on her back. Another Jack Henderson fan; he really was popular. A little tug of guilt for knowing nothing about the man or his football team gnawed at her gut, especially when Jack knew so much about her.

The woman in the jersey smiled. "Hi there, you must be new to the training sessions." But before Lauren could reply, which she wasn't really sure how to, the woman continued. "My son, Adam, is wearing the number three jersey." She pointed to a short, stocky boy who looked about ten. He was passing a football to another boy of about the same age who had a noticeable limp.

Lauren scanned the rest of the group of twelve boys and noticed they all appeared to have some form of physical impairment. The boy the woman next to her pointed to had Down syndrome, so did some of the others. Two boys had terrible limps, and the others had conditions that Lauren couldn't possibly identify.

Her heart broke as she thought of the struggles and hardships these beautiful boys must deal with every day. Not that you could tell by the smiles on their faces. They laughed and played like nothing could stop them. And when Jack came jogging onto the field, they yelled and whooped with excitement as if they were seeing the most famous man in the world.

"This is Adam's fourth training session. He's so excited about being trained by Jack Henderson," the jersey woman said. "Jack does such a wonderful job with the boys. He pays so much attention to them and has the patience of a saint. It's not easy getting twelve boys, especially ones with special needs, to pay attention for more than two seconds. But somehow Jack does." She looked over at her son. "Adam will never be a great footy player, but Jack makes him feel like he could play for Australia. The confidence these boys have after only four sessions is amazing. Jack is certainly more than a pretty face." She fanned her face and sighed. "But he sure is good to look at, especially in those little red shorts."

Jersey woman's words plunged deep inside Lauren. Not the comment about the red shorts, although he did look better than *good* in those, but because what he was doing for these boys proved he was more than just a pretty face.

How many times had she judged men by their looks? Too many times to count. And she had judged Jack the same way. He had turned out to be anything but a shallow, conceited, spoilt pretty boy. Yes, the outside packaging was beautiful, but the man inside looked just as good.

She didn't want to think about how it made her feel. She wasn't sure she was ready to let go of everything she believed was true, but he was making it damn hard to hold onto her beliefs.

The woman continued to chat, unaware of the struggle going through Lauren's mind. "Which one's your boy?" she asked, turning toward the field and scanning the boys. "Or hasn't he come on the field yet?"

Lauren shook her head. "I don't have a son training. I'm here with…" Her words trailed off. The woman had Jack's name on her...did Lauren really want to tell her she'd come with Jack? Instead she said, "I'm here with a friend."

Jersey woman glanced at the empty seat on the other

side of Lauren and raised a penciled eyebrow. "Does your friend have a son training?"

"Umm, no," Lauren said. Jersey woman fixed her gaze on Lauren, waiting for some kind of explanation. So she finally answered, "I came with Jack."

Both penciled eyebrows disappeared into her hairline. "You're here with Jack? Jack *Henderson*?"

Lauren shifted awkwardly in the seat, touched her locket, and nodded.

Jersey woman leaned forward and tapped the shoulders of two women sitting in front of them. They swiveled in their seats, both wearing curious expressions. "Ladies, this is…" Then she turned back to Lauren. "I'm sorry, I didn't get your name?"

Lauren hadn't given it to her. She could give her anything: Eve, Rachel, Fiona? But she reluctantly said, "Lauren."

Jersey woman turned back toward the two women and marveled, "This is Lauren. She's here with Jack *Henderson*!"

"Really?" one of the women said. She also wore a Flaming Star's jersey, but the name on the back of hers read *Campbell*. She pointed to Jack who had the boys sitting on the grass, their rapt expressions focused on him as he explained something to them. "*That* Jack Henderson?"

The one and only, and thank goodness there was only one of him; he was more trouble than she could handle. "Yes," she answered.

The woman wearing the Campbell jersey asked, "Is this a date?" Lauren's eyes grew wide.

Before Lauren could explain they were not there on a date the other woman sitting in front of them, who wore a very tight, black tank which pushed her boobs to a dangerous level of spilling out, spoke up. "He's taken you to watch him train a bunch of kids? So romantic." Sarcasm slid from her voice as she rolled her eyes and turned back around to face the football field.

Jersey woman leaned toward Lauren, covered her mouth, and whispered into her ear. "Don't listen to Karen. She's just jealous because Jack's never paid her any attention, no matter how slutty she dresses." Then in a louder voice, she said, "I think it's the perfect place for a date.

Watching Jack's toned legs run around in those shorts is the best date I could imagine."

"We're not—" she tried to explain but got cut off.

"He is taking you out to dinner afterward though, right?" Campbell jersey woman asked. Then she turned fully around in the seat and hooked her arm on the back of the chair, staring at Lauren as if waiting for her to tell them all about the exciting details.

"I bet he takes you to The Dunes, that's the most romantic restaurant around," Henderson jersey woman added.

"Ooh, that would be nice, but I'd love to imagine that Jack would take you back to his place and cook for you. He'd light candles and play soft music." Campbell jersey woman sighed blissfully then smiled with a wicked gleam. "And then you know where that would lead." She gave an exaggerated wink, causing both women to giggle like teenagers.

They were getting excited about a non-existent date. This was out of hand. She needed to put a stop to it.

Lauren blew out a long breath. "It's not a date. Jack and I are *friends*, nothing more."

Campbell jersey woman's face changed from excitement to disappointment. The woman named Karen with the too-small tank top sniggered loud enough for Lauren to hear.

"It's not a date?" Henderson jersey woman asked with an expression as if someone had told her Santa Clause wasn't real.

"It's not a date," Lauren reiterated, and because Henderson jersey woman looked so downcast, she added, "I'm sorry to disappoint you."

"Oh, well, that's a shame," Henderson jersey woman said. She nudged the back of Karen's shoulder with her finger. "Looks like there's still a chance for you then, eh, Karen?"

Karen swung her head back around, flicking her peroxide hair over her shoulder, and threw a dirty look at Henderson jersey woman.

It only made Henderson jersey woman laugh. Then she leaned toward Lauren again and said, "I'd be taking up the opportunity to get myself some of that man if I were you." She beamed.

Lauren shook her head. Did Jack turn all women into giant balls of lust ready to lie down and give their body up to him like a sacrifice to the gods? If these women—herself included, because let's face it, more than once she could have easily given it up for him—were any indication, she would say *hell yes*. She couldn't blame them. He really was sex on legs.

While the women, excluding Karen, were coming to terms with their disappointment, Jack jogged up the few stairs in the grandstand, put his foot up on the empty seat on the other side of Lauren, and rested his forearms on his thigh. "Lauren, I see you've met some of the boys' mums." He smiled at the women. "How are we all this afternoon, ladies?"

Jersey women Henderson and Campbell sat up straight in their seats, smiled like young girls, and answered in unison, "Great, Jack. How are you?" Lauren suppressed a laugh.

Fluffing out her damaged hair and puffing out a large chest, Karen answered in a sultry voice, "Fantastic now that you're here."

Ducking her head, Lauren rolled her eyes.

The smile Jack gave Karen was polite and showed no interest in whatever she was offering. Women had a habit of doing that around him.

He spoke briefly to the group about their boys, waved to a woman sitting a few seats away, and called out "How's it going?" to a couple of men standing at the railing around the field.

He looked down at Lauren with a playful grin. "Behave up here, honey. These lovely ladies think I'm a nice guy. Don't go telling them what you really think about me." He winked, leaned down, and smacked his lips on hers.

On a chorus of surprised gasps, hers included, he left and jogged back down the stairs and onto the grassy field. Her heart skidded to a stop. How was she going to explain herself out of this one?

All heads swiveled in her direction with surprised and accusatory expressions on their faces. Her face heated up as she struggled to find the words to explain what just happened. She had nothing. Besides, she didn't think they'd believe any explanations even if she did have full use of her voice.

Henderson and Campbell jersey women smiled at each other like they'd known what was really going on from the start. Karen huffed, picked up her bag from the floor, and moved over to where the others sat in the grandstand.

Jack called out to the boys, "Okay, men, let's train hard. I want to show my pretty lady what a great footy player I am."

Some boys whooped and whistled at Jack's comment while others groaned and made gagging noises. Jack laughed, scuffed the heads of the two boys closest to him, and then told them to run a lap of the field.

For the next hour Lauren watched him put the boys through their training drills. Jack ran along with the slower ones, praising them and cheering them on. He encouraged the boys who had trouble catching the ball to keep trying until eventually they did catch it. Their smiles lit up like Christmas lights at their achievement.

Not one of them complained they couldn't do something. Jack had made them believe they could achieve anything if they kept practicing. They worked hard, and Jack constantly praised them for it.

At the end, it was the boys' turn to put Jack through a few drills. They made him run three laps of the field, zigzag through orange cones, and do fifty push-ups and sit-ups. Jack groaned and complained that the boys were torturing him, but Lauren could tell he was doing it easily. And looked super-sexy doing it too. Henderson jersey woman hadn't been wrong about how good his tanned, muscled legs looked in those red training shorts. His ropey, strong arms when he threw a ball around made her think about wanting them wrapped around her.

Lauren's attention drifted back to the kids, and by their huge grins, she could tell they adored Jack. The happy expression on Jack's face as he high-fived each boy at the end of training said the feeling was mutual. Watching him train the boys with their physical challenges had been amazing. More than once a lump had formed in her throat while she witnessed how patient and kind he was with them. He was a good man who cared about the people around him.

How could Lauren have ever thought Jack was shallow when all he'd ever shown her was a caring side? Just look at how he had handled her crying lapses. Most men would have run away, not wanting to involve himself in the problems of someone he hardly knew. Yet Jack made her feel like he genuinely cared and wanted to help take away the pain.

And then she thought about the kiss earlier in the grandstand and how it threw her head into a spin. It wasn't a lust-fueled, toe-curling kiss like the ones before. It had been quick, sweet, and *claiming*. A kiss telling everyone 'this woman belongs to me'. And she wondered if that had been his intention. When they first met she would have thought it was a smooth trick to get what he wanted, but the more time they spent together she realized he cared and it was his way of showing it.

Damn, he was turning her emotions and everything she believed into a jumbled mess.

Chapter 22

*L*auren sat in Jack's car and waited while he showered and changed. All the boys and their parents had left, and she wondered if she could sneak in and take a peek. No one needed to know. It would be her dirty little secret. But she refrained herself from behaving like a Peeping Tom.

Ten minutes later Jack ambled out of the change rooms and headed toward his car. She saw a noticeable limp and remembered he had a football injury. He slid into the driver's seat, smelling of woodsy soap, and she had to stop herself from leaning into him to take a long, drawn-out sniff.

Throwing his bag onto the backseat, he started the car and drove out of the carpark. His dark, damp hair looked rumpled, like he had brushed it with his fingers, and droplets of water, illuminated by the dashboard's lights, glistened as they clung to his neck. He was the sexiest man she'd ever seen, and he also had a kind heart to go with it.

"Why did you have to turn out to be such a good guy?"

Flicking a quick, startled glance at her, he chuckled. "Should I apologize?"

She smiled. "I thought you were going to be a jerk. I wanted you to be a jerk. It would have made my life a lot easier."

"I'm not sure if that's a compliment, but in all fairness, not all guys in my situation are jerks. You never gave them a chance to show you otherwise."

He was right she thought as she stared out into the darkened streets. She never gave men like him a chance because she'd always been too scared. After what she had gone through with Graham it was easier to avoid any man who could ever put her in that kind of position again. Jack's big heart and kindness had helped open her eyes.

Jack took his eyes off the road as they stopped at a red light and flicked a heated gaze over her. "I'm happy you've never given other men a chance."

Her heart pounded against her ribs. "Oh?"

"Yeah, because some other guy would have you right now, and I wouldn't have a chance." His voice turned deep and husky. "Now I do."

Bubbles of excitement popped in her chest, but she tried to sound casual as she said, "What makes you think you have a chance now?"

The light turned green, and his gaze returned to the road but not before she saw his cocky grin. "Because I now know you have fallen for my irresistible personality." Waving her hand, she scoffed.

"Then it's my incredible athletic body you can't live without."

A laugh escaped her. "Oh, now you're really full of it. I'm just realizing you're not as bad as I first thought, so let's not get too carried away. You're not that hot," she teased. She wasn't going to tell him that he'd hit the nail on the head on both accounts, and he *really* was that *hot*.

His eyes grew round like he was in shock, but his lips twitched into a smile. "I'm not?"

She smacked him lightly on the arm, and he winced dramatically.

"Baby." She laughed.

"Hey, that arm has been throwing footy balls around all night."

"You were great with those kids. I could see they loved being there," she said in all seriousness.

"I love training them. They're a great bunch of boys. They only need someone to believe in them."

"You're a good guy, Jack. I'm sorry I judged you."

"I can still be very *bad*." He wiggled his eyebrows, and the dim interior did nothing to hide the devilish gleam in his eyes.

She couldn't help but smile back. No doubt he would be *bad* in the best possible way.

Jack drove them through Lauren's neighborhood, not back to her car like she thought he would. She was suddenly hit with a wave of panic. Her heart began to race, and her hands started to sweat. Should she thank him for helping her turn an ugly afternoon into a lovely one and then let him leave? Or invite him inside? For what? A drink? Dinner? Or… Her thoughts were playing ping-pong in her head. If he had taken her back to her car, she wouldn't have had to worry about making this decision.

So when he pulled onto her driveway she said, "You should have taken me back to my car."

"I'll have someone pick it up for you in the morning." He turned in his seat to face her.

Holding her bag in her lap and twisting the straps with wobbly fingers, she avoided the question she wanted to ask but didn't quite yet have the courage to. So instead she asked, "How did you know where I live?"

In a calm, quiet voice, the complete opposite to the jumble of jitteriness she was feeling, he whispered, "I know a lot about you." His hooded eyes turned dark like a summer storm as they searched her face. Did he know how he was affecting her?

God, he turned her into a nervous wreck with just one heated look. She dug deep to find the courage needed to ask, "Would you like to come upstairs?" When he didn't answer and looked at her intently she fiddled with her locket, averted her gaze, and continued on a nervous bubble of words. "We could order pizza or Chinese. Are you hungry? I'm starving. Are you hungry?" She mentally slapped her forehead. She'd already asked him that.

"Yes, I'm hungry." His gaze flicked to her mouth like he wanted *her* on the menu.

Opening the car door, she sprung out before she

could change her mind and send him home. Nothing needed to happen. It could just be two friends sharing a meal together. Nothing more. But her stomach did flip-flops, telling her she was a big fat liar.

On shaky legs, she climbed the stairs along the side of the garage leading up to her unit. The keys fumbled in her hand as she tried to stick it in the lock. She'd never brought a man home before. Jack had become many of her 'firsts'. After Graham, he was the first good-looking man she'd become attracted to, kissed, and had genuine feelings for. Thinking of the growing attraction and what may happen when they went inside caused her knees to shake and her heart to race.

Entering the small space of her unit, she flicked on the light and tossed her keys and bag on the coffee table. The already small room shrank with Jack's large presence. Jack looked around, and if he wondered why she lived in a small unit above a garage, he kept it to himself.

Lauren busied herself by searching through a pile of take-away brochures next to the phone and pulled out a random one. "Pizza okay with you?" God, her nerves were a jittery mess. Chest tight, she was finding it hard to breathe, like he was sucking the air out of the confined space.

Sauntering over to her, he glanced at the pizza place written on the brochure and screwed up his nose. "That stuff's no better than eating cardboard." She pulled out another one. "How about Chinese?" He shook his head.

"Burgers?"

"Do you want to clog up your arteries?" He shook his head again. "Please don't tell me you eat all this crap?"

She shrugged her shoulders. "I don't always have time to cook."

Jack ambled into the kitchen and stuck his head in the fridge. Rummaging around for a few seconds, he then pulled out tomatoes and placed them on the counter. "I'm surprised you're not fat or riddled with heart disease from eating that junk."

She dug her hands on her hips and tapped her foot as she watched him search, for God only knew what, in the pantry. "I'm not a big shot athlete like you who needs to stay in shape."

But she felt the need to defend herself. "I don't always eat this stuff." He cocked an eyebrow, not looking convinced. "You got any wine?" She pointed at a cupboard behind him.

Opening the door, he whistled and glanced over his shoulder at her. "Quite a good stash you have here."

The loaded cupboard held bottles of tequila, midori, vodka, and wine. Could she look any more like a junk food queen and an alcoholic? "I don't drink all of that myself." He made a face like he didn't believe her.

"I enjoy a drink or two with the girls. Nothing wrong with that."

He held up his hands. "No judgment." But mirth sparkled from his eyes.

"Why are you in my kitchen?" she said as she saw an array of ingredients spread out on the kitchen counter.

"Cooking dinner," he said as if to say *isn't it obvious?*

She remembered the conversation with the women at the football field.

"I'd love to imagine that Jack would take you back to his place and cook for you. He'd light candles and play soft music. And then you know where that would lead."

Except this wasn't Jack's house, and there were no candles or soft music. She clung on to the small details.

Jack put spaghetti on to boil, sautéed tomato and garlic, and had the kitchen smelling as good as an Italian restaurant. And watching Jack standing in her kitchen cooking dinner was the most delicious thing she could imagine. Her mouth watered, and it wasn't because of the food.

"When did you learn to cook?" she asked as she busied herself setting the table, holding herself back from lighting the candle that sat in the center of the table.

He scooped a teaspoon into the sauce and tasted it, added a sprinkle of pepper and a splash of red wine, and then went on to pour them both a glass. "I can cook enough to keep me away from the take-away places you enjoy." He smirked.

She rolled her eyes, and he laughed.

As she watched Jack move around the kitchen, the limp she'd noticed after training had not gone away. Pointing at his leg, she asked, "Is your knee giving you problems?"

He rubbed it like he'd just noticed it and shrugged. "No more than usual."

He leaned back against the kitchen counter and crossed his legs at the ankle, the movement bringing his package, which was now clad in faded tight denim, to her attention. She tried to keep her focus on his knee, but it was difficult.

"Would you like ice?" She walked to the fridge to get some from the freezer, but he stopped her.

"Not necessary. It's not so bad."

She sat down at the table. "I know you injured your knee during a game…"

One eyebrow rose questioningly. Jack knew Lauren had little knowledge of his time playing football.

So she said, "Jade," which was sufficient explanation. "How did it happen?"

He emptied his wineglass with one last swallow and placed it on the table. "I went in for a tackle and blew out my knee." He bent and rubbed the old injury. "I missed the rest of the season, and when I recovered my knee was never the same. I couldn't give my team one-hundred percent. So I retired."

"That's a shame. Do you think you'd still be playing today if it didn't happen?"

Jack stirred the sauce and took it off the heat. "For a while I thought I'd be playing into my late thirties. I convinced myself I was invincible and could still be a key player for the team.

But then I cleared the bullshit from my eyes and knew reaching thirty and still having the success I had was incredible." He drained the spaghetti and poured the rich-smelling sauce over the pasta.

"Do you miss it?" she asked as she refilled their wineglasses.

"I'm still around the game enough to feel like I haven't given it up completely. It's enough for me." He dished the pasta into two bowls and carried them to the table. "And to be honest, I'm kind of glad I don't have such a grueling workout schedule. I don't have the energy for it anymore." He tapped his stomach. "I've let myself go."

Lauren scoffed and rolled her eyes. "Yes, you need to do something about that." Jack laughed at her sarcasm.

They sat in silence as they devoured the delicious tasting meal. Then Jack pointed his fork at the fridge and asked, "Who's the older woman in the photo with you and your friends?"

She turned her head to the fridge. "That's Lillian. She lives in the house out front. She's gone to Europe for two months with her two sons."

"You look close."

In the photo Lauren had her arms wrapped around Lillian's shoulders. Lillian's dark brown head was touching Lauren's and their cheeks pressed together. They both smiled widely at the camera.

"We are. She's like a mother to me." Lillian had only been away a month, but Lauren missed her terribly and was counting down the days until she came home.

Standing, Lauren picked up their empty plates, rinsed them in the sink, and wiped the counter. When she'd run out of things to keep busy, she sat back down at the table. Jack hadn't said anything about the way he'd found her outside of the coffee shop, but she could tell he was still waiting for an explanation.

Lauren took a deep breath. "I met with my sister

Belinda today. She came to collect money for my mother's medical bills and to tell me my mother died and had already been buried. I told her she should've called me, but Belinda didn't think I needed to know. She only wanted me to pay for it." She shredded a napkin in her hand. "I don't know if I would have gone to the funeral, but Belinda took that choice away from me."

Jack slid his hand along the table, but she pulled away and placed her hands in her lap.

Being comforted for the loss of someone she didn't really care about felt wrong.

He raised an eyebrow when she pulled away, but he didn't comment about it. "She should have told you. You needed to make that decision for yourself, but it's over now. You don't need to see Belinda ever again."

A short, bitter sound came out of Lauren's mouth. "I still need to give her more money or she'll…" She bit her lip to stop herself from saying anything else.

"Or she'll what?"

The chair made a loud scraping noise as she pushed it back from the table. Standing, she

paced the small kitchen. Jack blocked her and put his hands on her shoulders.

"Or she'll what?" he asked again, his voice low and serious.

With a deep, shuddery breath she answered, "Or she'll sell my sordid story about Graham to the media."

Jack frowned. "Why would she do that?"

"It's what she does, calls and asks for money, and if I

don't give it to her, she threatens to go the media with what she knows."

"She's blackmailing you?" An expression as dark as thunder clouds grew over his face.

Looking away, she nodded.

"How long has this been going on?" The words were soft but laced with acid.

"She started demanding money after she found out I was pregnant with Graham's baby." Blowing out a breath, Jack let go of her shoulders and ran his fingers through his hair. "Let her go to the media. Who cares if Graham Stone's squeaky-clean reputation is ruined? After the pain the bastard put you through he deserves to be ruined."

"It's not that simple." Crossing her arms over her chest, she rubbed them like it was a chilly winter's day. "It's my reputation too. I've worked hard for what I have. If this got out, there's no doubt in my mind Graham would portray me as the one who threw myself at him and tried to wreck a happy marriage."

A muscle twitched in his clenched jaw as he spoke through tight lips. "No one would believe that."

She scoffed. "Graham is Australia's top journalist and he's climbing the ladder overseas. My God, I hear he's friends with Oprah. Of course people will believe him over a small gift shop owner looking for five minutes of fame."

His dark expression didn't change.

She cupped his face in her hands. "Thank you for caring so much."

His eyes softened, but his lips remained in a tight line. Pulling him toward her, she placed a light kiss on his lips. It was only meant to be a friendly 'thank you' kiss. But as she pulled back and looked into his piercing green eyes that burned through to her soul, she needed to pull him back for more. Any more questions would have to wait. She wanted to forget the past and concentrate on the present. Concentrate on the man standing so strong and warm in front of her.

She wrapped her arms around his neck and pressed her body up against him. He groaned, and she felt him harden against her stomach. She quivered, and her body melted around him.

Jack's lips found the side of her neck, and he slid his tongue along the sensitive skin. Heat shot wild fire through Lauren's veins, and her breathing grew choppy. Closing her eyes, she tilted her head to the side.

His hands traveled in a slow, blistering trail up the side of her body, and as he reached her breasts he brushed his fingertips underneath the curve. A tingling sensation shot through her breasts, causing her nipples to peak as she waited for more. As if reading her mind, he cupped them in his hands and stroked his thumbs over the raised buds. She sighed, but it sounded more like a groan, and every nerve ending sizzled with the heat their bodies generated. The sensation explosion too much for Lauren to take.

Jack backed her against the wall, the extra support helpful if she wanted to stay on her feet, lowered his head, and replaced his hand with his mouth. Trembling, she inhaled sharply. God, she would have thought she'd died and gone to heaven but his mouth was anything but holy. It was thoroughly sinful.

As Jack continued to suck and nibble, the warm wetness of his tongue dampened the thin fabric of her top. His hand then descended a slow and torturous path to another hot spot. When his fingers found their mark, her legs gave way. Jack wrapped an arm around her waist just in time to catch her before she melted into a puddle of jelly on the floor.

As Jack steadied her on shaky feet, his quick, nibble fingers flicked open her blouse and bra. Closing his eyes, he drew in a couple of breaths, like he needed a moment to keep himself together. After a few painfully long seconds he lowered his head and covered her breast with his warm mouth. Lauren cried out and arched toward the tongue circling her nipple.

"God, you're beautiful." The sound of his voice was rough and sexy.

He picked her up, and of their own free will, her legs wrapped around his waist and her breasts pushed up to his face. But instead of taking her up against the wall like she thought he was going to do—something she wouldn't have complained about—he made the few steps into the living room and dropped her on the couch.

For a moment he stood over her, his breathing deep and raspy like he'd just run up ten flights of stairs. Her top was open, her breasts exposed, and his heated gaze traveling over her body filled her with satisfaction. Making no effort to cover up, she reveled in the dark, hooded expression on his face.

She could tell by Jack's clenched jaw that he was holding back, giving her a moment to decide whether to go through with it. A hundred reasons why she should put a stop to it ran through her mind. Would he walk away after he'd gotten what he'd wanted? Could her heart cope if that happened? But she wanted him, so much so that if he didn't join her on the couch soon she would climb up him. Actually, that sounded like a great idea.

She caught his hand and pulled him closer, but he still didn't lie down with her.

"Are you sure you want to do this?" It sounded like it strained him to ask.

Was she sure? Yes.

Would she have regrets? Maybe.

But right then her mind had closed for the day and her body was open for business. In answer to his question, she dug her fingers in the waistband of his jeans. He sucked in a shaky breath as she pulled him on top of her.

He chuckled as he landed on her, but as soon as their mouths fused together, the laughter turned into a low, hungry growl. Her hands trembled as they traveled down the length of his hard body. When she found the zipper of his jeans his muscles tightened, and Lauren was happy to find he'd gone commando. Lifting his erection out of his jeans, she slowly stroked the hard length.

Dropping his head onto her shoulder, he sucked in a jagged breath. "You're killing me. I wanted to take my time with you, but if you keep touching me like that, I'm afraid it will be over before the good stuff starts."

"It gets better?" She bit him playfully on the chin. "I can't wait."

"You will have to wait until round two because I need to be inside you now!" A vein pulsed as he clenched his jaw.

Her body vibrated with excitement at the promise of doing this more than once. Their hands were a blur as they removed only the clothing that restricted the access they needed.

A condom seemed to appear out of thin air and he rolled it on. He entered her fast and hard, and Lauren cried out. Stopping, Jack's body stiffened above her. A frown creased his forehead as he looked down at her.

"Are you okay?" He gritted his teeth. She could see it was taking all his self-control to keep still.

Nodding, she wrapped her legs around his waist and pulled him closer. Needing no more encouragement, he pumped hard and fast inside her, and Lauren matched him stroke for stroke. Soon her body trembled and buckled underneath him until the pressure built into an explosion of monumental proportions and she cried out her release. Jack pumped into her one last time before he collapsed on top of her, his breathing loud and raspy.

Lauren lay still underneath the heavy, yet pleasant, weight of Jack. Their wet skin glued them together, and their choppy breathing mingled as one. *Wow* was the only thought Lauren's sex-starved brain could manage right before she dozed off.

Chapter 23

Sunlight filtered through the slats of the blinds, striping Lauren's bed with golden streaks.

Lauren's eyes, heavy from lack of sleep, opened to sort out the weight anchored around her waist. She found Jack's tanned, muscled arm secured around her. Stretching carefully, so as not to wake him, she smiled like the cat that got the cream. Her body tingled in places she'd long forgotten, and it felt wonderful. And it was all thanks to the man lying in her bed.

She turned her head to gaze at him. Jack's dark eyelashes fanned the tops of his cheeks as he slept. His hair, disheveled from her fingers running through it, looked sexy and rugged. Stubble covered his jaw, and she remembered how rough, yet arousing, it felt on her sensitive skin. The sting still lingered on her neck and breasts.

Her gaze wandered down the length of his body. The photos of his Calvin Klein shoot did not give the man justice. He was so much sexier in the flesh. A sprinkle of dark hair splayed across his broad, muscular chest and a *happy trail*, which she had followed more than once with her tongue, disappeared beneath the rumpled sheet covering him from the waist down.

Looking at him caused her heart to race and her breath to catch, and she realized the trouble with *Mr. Pretty* was going to be bigger than she ever could have imagined. It hadn't taken her long to get hooked. What was she saying? She'd been hooked from the beginning. And now that she'd gotten a taste of this delicious man the craving grew wildly stronger. Lauren was like a junkie waiting for her next hit.

Thank God she didn't have to wait long. His warm fingers slid their way up her body, boldly cupping her breast and massaging it in a slow, tantalizing circle. Goose bumps broke out over her skin, and she bit her lip to keep from moaning. How could it still feel so damn good after all they'd done? Jack continued with his expert touch and her body, of its own accord, arched into his palm.

Jack's lids fluttered open. "Morning," he said, his voice deep and raspy from sleep.

"Morning," Lauren answered on a sigh when his fingers began to pluck at her nipples.

"Sleep well?" Leaning over, he covered her breast with his warm mouth.

On a low groan she answered, "Ah-huh."

The hand left her breast and headed south. Lauren sucked in a breath as he entered a finger through her slick heat. She rocked fast against him as he flicked and pulled at the sensitive bud that controlled her body. Boy, he knew his way around her controls!

Rolling on top of her, Jack pinned her down, linked their fingers, and slid her arms above her head, exposing her to his heated gaze. He nudged her legs open and nestled between them.

She wiggled, urging him to enter, but he only stared down at her with his smoky green eyes.

Groaning deep in her throat, she lifted her head and took an impatient bite from his shoulder.

"What's the rush?" Lowering his mouth, he nibbled at her bottom lip.

Lauren wrapped her legs around his waist and pulled him as close as she could without the use of her arms. "Jack…"

"I can't get enough of you," he muttered as he once again paid tribute to her chest.

Coming to the end of her patience, Lauren pulled her hands free and clasped them on Jack's face and glared at him. "If you don't get the job done now, I'm going to…going to…"

His eyes sparkled with laughter. "Going to what?"

"Finish things myself!" she blurted.

The sparkle was replaced by scorching heat. "I'd be *very* happy to see that." She blew out a frustrated breath. Threats weren't going to work.

"Say *please*." His hot gaze flicked over her.

"What?"

"Say *please, Jack, I want you right now*," he said with a cocky grin.

Was he seriously going to do this to her now? When she was on the verge of shattering?

Narrowing her eyes, she said, "You can't be serious."

Ignoring her, he said, "Say *please, Jack, I want you now, because you're the best lover I've ever had.*"

He was right about being the best lover she'd ever had, but she wasn't dumb enough to tell him, so Lauren pressed her lips tight and shook her head.

"No?" His eyes widened with a mischievous gleam, and he lowered his head and licked a raised nipple. After a few teasing moments he lifted his head and cocked an eyebrow. "Are you going to say it?" His voice shook. This punishment affected Jack too.

She shook her head, although standing her ground was pure torture.

The mischievous gleam flashed back in his green eyes, and that only meant trouble.

He began to slide inside her, and for a moment, she believed it was all too much for him too and he'd given up on tormenting her. She blew out a sigh of relief. Then, too quickly, he pulled away. Lauren wanted to groan, scream, punch him. But Jack's jaw clenched and she was happy to see that his little mind game wasn't so easy on him either.

With strength Lauren didn't think she had left, she pushed Jack onto his back. The look of surprise on his face gave her a burst of satisfaction. She straddled his lap, making sure she gave a good wiggle on his arousal. He threw back his head and cursed. Two could play dirty tricks. This time it was Lauren's turn for mind games.

Taking a page from his dirty book, and gathering all

the self-control she could muster, she pinned his hands above his head, making sure her breasts were inches from his mouth. His eyes hooded and his head lifted to reach them, but she pulled back. Dropping his head back on the pillow, he groaned. She knew he could easily flip her back over and she'd be at his mercy again, but he was letting her have some fun.

"Say *please, Lauren, I want you now, because you're the best lover I've ever had.*" She mimicked him, giving him some of his own medicine. She gave another wiggle.

He blew out a shaky laugh. "Please, Lauren, I want you now, because you're the best lover I've ever had." He shrugged. "What can I say? I want to get laid bad, and these games are fucking with my mind."

"And I had so much torture planned for you." She released his hands and slid her fingers up her ribcage and cupped her breasts.

He growled and flipped them over. "Fuck, I wanna see you continue with that after I'm done."

Fumbling with a condom left on the nightstand, he rolled it on and knelt between her legs. Gripping her hips, he entered her fully. Gasping, she dropped her head back and rocked against him on a wave of pure ecstasy. They'd both won the game.

ack pushed himself until his body dripped sweat and his legs burned, clocking up one hour on the treadmill. He had a small room at the back of the shop set up with gym equipment so he could exercise whenever the mood struck. Exercise always cleared his head and got his thoughts straight, but it wasn't working.

Still buzzed after the long hours spent in Lauren's bed, he'd come to the office early but couldn't concentrate on the work he needed to catch up on or the documents Ellen needed him to finalize. The spreadsheets opened on his computer screen were a blur, and he couldn't focus on the invoices on his desk waiting for his attention, so he decided he'd burn some energy at the gym.

Women had always been available, and he had his fair share. Many of them were easily forgettable. Several left a fond memory but none that consumed his mind. Lauren had left her mark in a way no other woman had ever done before, and the fact that he liked it surprised him. He liked Lauren in a big way and wanted to see where their connection would lead. Another big surprise.

For years his motto was to 'never get involved' but now he *wanted* to get involved with Lauren, and it didn't scare him like he thought it would.

Pushing himself for another twenty minutes until his legs began to shake, he turned off the machine before his face met with the rubber of the treadmill. Pulling a towel off a chair, he rubbed the sweat off his face and neck, and grabbed a bottle of water from the mini-fridge.

Jack had now accepted he couldn't continue with the football lifestyle he once led, and truthfully, he hadn't wanted it for a while. It took Lauren to crash into his life to make him realize it.

Jack wanted to leave his past behind him to be a better man for Lauren. She made him *believe* he could be a better man. And the more time they spent together showed him a relationship was possible. Now he just needed to convince Lauren to put away her painful past and open her heart to the possibilities of something more with him.

Lauren and her issue with *Mr. Pretty* was the stumbling block. Jack knew she didn't compare him anymore, but this morning, as he drove her to her car, he could sense her pulling away, slowly building the wall back up. For a few hours she'd let go, but once the sexual haze cleared, he could see reality struck her in the face and she retreated.

Did she regret their time together? He sure as hell

didn't, and he would not let her shut him out and crawl back into her protective shell. He'd blown her *Mr. Pretty* theory well and truly out of the water and she could no longer use it as a shield. Convincing her to take the leap together wouldn't be easy, but he was all about hard work and persistence.

***

Lauren's constant flow of customers kept her busy. Jaime had Saturday mornings off, so Lauren was required on the floor to serve. She was grateful for the distraction. Work kept her mind, most of the time, from thinking about Jack.

The night's activities still had the power to make her skin heat when she thought about it. It had been the best night of her life. A night she'd always remember. Memories she'd pull out and relive over and over again, reminding her of a time when she once opened up and experienced all there was with a man like Jack.

Even though Lauren could no longer compare Jack to a typical *Mr. Pretty*, she knew what happened could never happen again. He was still 'Jack Henderson', Australia's much loved sports star. A lump formed in her throat and her hand shook as she organized the photo frames on the shelf. It was the only way. There would always be cameras, stories, and groupies. A life she wouldn't expect him to walk away from, but a life she couldn't fit into.

The door opened and another customer entered before Lauren could examine her reactions further. Not one to pounce on a customer as soon as they entered, she gave the woman time to wander around the shop while she busied herself tidying up the shelf of photo frames.

When she had given her enough time to browse Lauren approached her. "Good morning. Can I help you with anything?" She noticed the glass candlestick in the woman's hand. "All candlesticks are twenty percent off."

The woman brushed her long chestnut hair off her shoulder and said, "Thanks, but I'm only looking." Her painted red smile appeared cold and unfriendly.

Lauren knew not all customers wanted help. "If you need anything, just let me know." The phone rang and she excused herself to answer it.

Jack's name appeared on the screen and her heart hammered against her chest. She took a deep breath to calm her jittery nerves before answering. "Jack."

"Hello, Lauren." Her name spoken in his low, deep voice sent a blast of heat to her girly parts that, only a few hours ago, he'd paid special attention to. "I have a package waiting here for your attention."

Gasping, she looked over her shoulder at the customer, and whispered into the phone, "I gave your *package* enough of my attention last night *and* this morning." It had given her many hours of pleasurable entertainment.

She shook herself; she couldn't think about it, otherwise, with her girly parts throbbing their consent, she'd be tempted to go running back for more. It was tough, but she'd already decided that last night was a one-night deal.

His deep chuckle vibrated through the phone. "As

much as I loved your thorough attention, and would be happy for more, I have an *actual* package here for you. You know, as in a delivery."

Lauren slapped her forehead, and her face burned hot. "I'm such an idiot."

"Nah, it's only natural after the night we had for you to be thinking about *my* package."

Lauren choked on a laugh. "Oh, you are so full of it, Jack Henderson," she said, then gave a quick glance at the customer.

The woman was staring in her direction, but as soon as Lauren turned toward her, she averted her gaze back to the display of candlesticks. Lauren noticed an angry expression on her face before she turned away. She probably wanted help now and was upset because Lauren was on the phone. Customers could be funny about things like that.

"Jack, I have a customer. I need to go."

"What about the package? Will you come by the office to take a look?"

Did Jack sound eager to see her again? A bubble of excitement built, but she squashed it back down just as quick. She had decided she wouldn't be taking things any further. Last night had been fun—a lot of fun. But fun could turn into dangerous territory for her if she continued.

"Where's the package from?" she asked.

Jack was silent for a moment, and she heard a rustling sound through the phone.

"Officeworks."

"It's a box of stationary. You don't need me for that."

"I don't know what to do with it."

Was he playing the dumb card just so he could get her to his office? The bubble of excitement blew up a little bigger and was harder to ignore.

"It's pens, paper clips, that sort of thing. Put them in the drawers of your desk."

"But—"

A crash vibrated through the shop. Lauren whipped her head toward the sound. Tiny pieces of glass lay scattered at the customer's feet. "Oh no! Jack, I have to go."

"Lauren, wait—"

Lauren hung up, cutting Jack off, and rushed toward the woman.

"Whoops!" the woman said as she stepped away from the broken candlesticks. The glass crunched under her black heels. Five sets of candlesticks lay smashed on the tiled floor, the shelf they had sat on now empty.

"Are you hurt?" Lauren searched the woman's bare legs for any sign of blood. Relief washed over her when she saw none.

"No, but your candlesticks have seen better days," the woman said with a twisted smile, and her smoky gray eyes appeared to gleam with excitement. "You should get the shelf looked at, it's unstable."

The woman actually looked happy about the damage. Lauren was at a loss for words.

"I've made such a mess." The woman kicked a chunk of crystal with the toe of her black pumps.

There was something cagey about the lady and Lauren

wanted her out of the shop. It wasn't the first time she'd had breakages, but it was the first one of this size, and the first time someone hadn't felt any remorse or offered to pay for damages.

"It won't take me long to clean up," Lauren remarked.

"I'll leave you too it then." Smiling smugly, she wiggled her fingers, then left.

Lauren stood in shock and watched her go. What on earth was her problem? She had a feeling the smashed candlesticks hadn't been an accident. From the moment the woman had entered the shop, Lauren had felt a wave of hostility roll off her, but why?

She shook herself out of her musings. She needed to clean up before someone walked in and hurt themselves.

Chapter 25

*A*fter an exhausting two hours of exercise, Jack still couldn't get Lauren out of his mind. He'd had to think up a lame excuse to call her so he could arrange to see her again. What happened to the days when he'd call a woman and arrange a place and time to meet with no explanation needed? It stopped the day he met Lauren Moore.

When Jack heard a loud crash at Lauren's shop and the worried sound of her voice right before she hung up, he knew he had to get to her right away. His workout gear was still damp, and it stuck to him as he ran to his car and pulled out onto the busy street. It took him half the time it should have to get to Lauren's shop, and he wouldn't be surprised if he received a couple of speeding fines from the speed cameras he'd passed on the way.

Parking in front of Everything Nice, Jack hurried inside. He found Lauren on her hands and knees with glass scattered all around her. "Lauren!"

"Jack, what are you doing here?" Her eyes rounded with surprise.

Squatting, he grabbed hold of her wrists. With so much broken glass around he had expected to find her covered in blood. After a quick inspection, finding no blood in sight, he released a long, held breath. A wave of relief rolled over him but he needed to ask to make sure.

"Are you hurt? Are you bleeding anywhere?" Maybe he'd missed something.

"Yes, I am bleeding," she answered.

Again, he scanned her exposed skin, looking for blood.

She laughed. Frowning, he met her gaze.

Lauren pointed her index finger. A tiny spec of blood marred her pale skin. "I cut myself sweeping up the glass. Should I call an ambulance?" Her lips twitched.

Looking at the injured finger from different angles, Jack gave it a thorough inspection.

"Hmmm, doesn't appear to be too deep. Although I do believe it requires medical attention."

"It does?" Lauren's eyes widened with mock concern.

"Yes, it does," Jack answered with all seriousness. "Good thing I'm trained for injuries like this." Pulling the finger to his lips, he placed a soft kiss on the tip. "There, it should feel better now."

Lauren gazed at her finger like Jack had performed a miracle. "I'm healed! Thank you so much, kind sir."

"I don't work for free. I will require payment."

She batted her eyelashes. "Payment? How can I pay you?"

The endless erotic ways she could repay him paraded through his mind. He hardened as he envisioned Lauren, naked and glistening from sweat, on his bed as payment pending.

Holding onto her hands, he pulled her up and stepped them away from the glass. "My services are very expensive."

She touched her locket and bit her bottom lip. It wasn't hard to see her mind working, trying to decide if she should play along or back off. God, he prayed she wanted to play.

Jack saw the moment when she'd made up her mind and then, to his fucking delight, she slid her arms around his neck and raised her face to him, their lips almost touching. "Name your price."

Removing her hands from around his neck, he stepped away. Her disappointed expression would have made him laugh if he wasn't so turned on.

Swinging the *closed* sign on the door, he flicked the lock and ambled back to her. "Now, about that payment," he said right before claiming her lips, backing her into her office, and kicking the door shut.

Chapter 26

*L*auren's warm, sweaty body stuck to the hard length of Jack's side. Their legs tangled together, their breathing heavy. It hadn't taken much for Jack to get her naked and in his kingsize bed.

After he'd backed her into her office and taken her up against the wall, he'd bundled her into his car and headed for his house. She'd tried unconvincingly to tell him that she couldn't just shut up shop; she had a business to run. But he ignored her feeble excuses, pushed her out the door, and had her purring like his luxury sports car in record time.

She knew she should have stopped him. Had convinced herself it wouldn't happen again. But she justified her lack of self-control by telling herself she'd needed this one last day with him before she moved on. Her heart pounded and filled with emotions she needed to shut down before she dived into them and drowned. She reached for her locket, a strong reminder of the consequences if she invested her heart completely.

Touching her fingers, Jack stopped her fidgeting and held the locket in his hand. The tarnished silver, in his palm, looked small and delicate. "I've never seen you without this, and I don't know if you realize it, but you constantly touch it. Especially when you're uncomfortable or you have something on your mind." He dropped the locket and cupped her face in his hands.

"I know you're not feeling uncomfortable." His heated gaze slid down her exposed, naked body. "So I'm guessing you've got something on your mind, and judging by the seriousness on your face, you're not thinking about the pornographic things you still want to do to me."

Lauren chuckled, trying to laugh at his joke, but she failed miserably. Jack tilted her face up toward him, and his eyes bore into hers, willing her to open up to him.

"This locket is a cheap piece of jewelry I found at a seaside market. It's what's inside that's priceless." Her voice wavered. "It holds a lock of Abby's hair."

Jack pulled her in closer and kissed her forehead.

"It's a reminder of how much I've lost. After losing Abby I needed something tangible, something I could see and touch to keep me from falling into the same trap." Feeling Jack stiffen, she glanced up at him and gasped with surprise at the fierce frown on his face.

"And you still think I'm a trap?"

She shook her head. "No, but we both know it's not forever." He opened his mouth to speak, but she cut in before he could say something he didn't really mean but thought that she wanted to hear. "It's okay. It is what it is. You've been exactly what I needed to open my eyes and start living again." She kissed the side of his jaw. "Thank you."

He untangled himself and rose from the bed. Although the room was balmy, she shivered from the absence of his body heat.

Jack shoved his legs into a pair of black boxer briefs, turned to face her, and dug his hands on his hips. "Did you just *thank* me?"

"Yes?" Her voice rose on the word like a question.

"You're thanking me for releasing you from the *Mr. Pretty* trap? So now that you're *cured* you're open to relationships with men who happen to be successful and-or good-looking?"

She hadn't exactly put it that way. He wasn't the commitment kind of guy. Shouldn't he be happy she wasn't expecting more?

"No, don't answer that. I don't want to know." He picked up his discarded jeans she'd had the pleasure of removing earlier and tugged them on. Opening a drawer, he pulled out a clean black t-shirt and pulled it on.

Lauren rose from the bed, wrapped the sheet around her body, and scanned the room for her clothes. It looked like her time with Jack was truly over. Her heart sank to the pit of her stomach. This was what she wanted. She only wished it didn't have to end on bad terms.

She put her clothes on and searched for her shoes. Jack picked them up from under the bed and handed them to her, his shuttered expression unreadable. A lump formed in her throat and threatened to suffocate her.

"Jack…" Her voice cracked on his name. She couldn't find the words to say goodbye.

"Let's go."

Pulling into the parking lot behind Lauren's building, Jack parked next to her car. Her tires had been slashed, and spray painted on the bonnet was the word *slut*.

A bunch of colorful profanity spewed from Jack's mouth as he stormed out of his car, slamming the door behind him. Wanting to get a closer look, Lauren hurried out and joined Jack.

His phone was pressed to his ear as he spoke with the police.

Circling the car, she took in the damage. The Toyota Corolla wasn't anything fancy, but she took pride in looking after it.

Lifting a hand to shade her eyes against the sun, she scanned the parking lot, not really sure what she was searching for, but the small parking area reserved for her and Jaime's cars was empty.

Someone had come to her place of work and vandalized her car. An icy shiver traveled up her spine. "Who would do this to my car?"

Jack ended his call and put the phone in his pocket. "There's a police officer in the area. They'll be here soon."

"Who would do this?" she repeated, not expecting

Jack to have the answers. But when she saw the guilt-ridden expression, she knew he did. "You know, don't you?"

Jack was saved from answering when a police car pulled into the carpark. An officer with thinning salt-and-pepper hair emerged from the vehicle. He pulled the waist of his pants over a sagging belly and adjusted his gun belt.

Placing his hands on Lauren's shoulders, Jack said, "Let me deal with this. Can you please wait for me over at the coffee shop? I'll explain everything after I talk to the officer."

"But…it's my car. I should stay."

"Please, Lauren." Something in his eyes begged her to do what he asked.

She agreed, and made her way to the coffee shop across the street and ordered two coffees to go. Finding a vacant table next to the window, she sat down to wait for her order and watched Jack and the officer as they inspected her car. The officer pulled out a little black book, nodded as Jack spoke, and wrote in the book. They spoke for a couple more minutes, shook hands, and the officer got back in his car and drove away.

Jack looked for a break in traffic, then crossed the street.

Lauren paid for the coffees, met him outside the café, and handed him his cup.

In a calm, quiet tone that belied his stiff expression, he said, "We need to talk."

The sober words made Lauren's stomach tightened. "Yes, we do."

Chapter 27

Walking side by side, Jack and Lauren sipped their coffees while gathering their thoughts. The boutiques in the surrounding area had closed for the day. Only the cafés and restaurants stayed open past two o'clock on a Saturday afternoon.

They continued to walk until they reached a small park. Banksia trees surrounded the perimeter, dappling the lush, green grass with afternoon sunlight. They found a bench seat under the shade to get out of the afternoon heat. Four young children laughed as they swung on the swings and flew down the slippery dip.

Jack knew Lauren was waiting for him to tell her who had ruined her car. How the fuck did Claire known he was involved with Lauren? The problem with Claire had become more serious than he'd anticipated. He was not okay with the bitch involving Lauren in her vendetta against him.

Running his hand through his hair, Jack blew out a

breath. Over the past few weeks Lauren had let go of her insecurities and opened up. Sure, she wanted to believe Jack had been her very own sex therapist and she was now able to go and face all the *Mr. Prettys* in town. As much as he hated to think about it, she could have any man she wanted. And it killed him to imagine her with anyone else.

His eyes connected with her unreadable expression. Her hair, which had been tied up in a neat bun when he entered her shop earlier in the day, was now in a loose ponytail. A few tendrils danced around her face with the breeze. A funny kind of thud happened in his chest. The feelings for her were stronger than he had ever had before. There was no denying that. And he cared too much to hide the truth from her. Dammit, he didn't want to be another man in her life who lied.

"I know who damaged your car," he said.

"I know you do."

He winced at her clipped tone.

"Whoever wrecked your office decided my car was going to be their next masterpiece."

She turned and glared at him. "I want to know why."

Jack scrubbed his hand over his face. "Earlier in December, when Leah went on maternity leave, I needed help in the office, so I hired a woman named Claire. She stayed back late one night after work and we..." He cleared his throat. "Stuff happened."

"You had sex."

Shame weighed his shoulders down. "I regretted it straight away. I knew it was a stupid thing to do."

He paused for a beat, hoping that she'd say 'these things happen' and she understood. But she sat as still as stone, so he continued.

"I tried to explain to her it had been a big mistake and it could never happen again, but she…let's just say, didn't take it well. She told me I'd regret treating her that way. And she didn't wait long to make good on her threat. After she destroyed my office she slashed the tires of my car."

Lauren raised an eyebrow. He had kept that part from her, and she didn't look impressed.

"I thought she'd finished with her revenge, but now she's involved you. I don't know how she found out about us. I'm so sorry."

Jack reached for her hand, but she pulled it away, and he sighed. He could see the trust they'd slowly built slipping away.

"And because she's now involved you, I had to tell the police. Hopefully they'll find her."

Lauren scoffed. "The police have better things to do with their time than find a pissed off woman with a spray can." She picked up her bag from the seat and placed the strap on her shoulder. "I need to go."

Jack reached for her hand again, and she jumped off the seat like she had springs on her ass. "Don't go. We need to talk about this. Claire was a mistake. She never should have involved you. Her issues are with me."

She threw her hands up in frustration. "That's the problem, Jack, she did involve me."

Rising, Jack tried to place calming hands on her

shoulders, but she took a step back. He sighed, and his arms fell to his sides.

Her hand fidgeted with her locket, and he watched as she held onto it like a lifeline. He wanted to reach for her fingers and steady them but knew she wouldn't let him.

"She's reminded me that you were always going to be a bad idea."

He suppressed a sigh of frustration. "Lauren, you're upset… I'll handle Claire, and this won't ever happen again."

She gave a mirthless laugh. "Of course it will happen again. Your history doesn't show many long-lasting relationships, Jack. Have they ever lasted more than a night?" She began to pace in front of him and continued without waiting for an answer. "Surely there are other women out there that you've brushed aside without any concern for their feelings. Or maybe a jealous ex-lover will come out with a juicy story about you. Like maybe…" She looked around as if she was trying to find inspiration then clicked her fingers when an idea struck. "A baby you knew nothing about."

He pinched the bridge of his nose and closed his eyes for a second to keep calm. "How many times have I told you I'm not Graham?"

"I know you're not Graham, but I can't live like this, knowing that somewhere out there is a woman—and who knows how many more—who can invade my life like this. I have enough drama to deal with, I don't need yours too."

She turned to leave. This time he caught her arm and

pulled her to a stop. "My history isn't squeaky-clean. I've done a lot of dumb shit, I can't change that. But I want more than a night or two with you. I've never wanted anyone the way I want you, and it scares the hell out of me."

She searched his face, and he hoped she saw the truth of his words and gave him a chance.

"But do you know what scares me more?" He didn't wait for a reply. "What scares me more is that you'll walk away from me without giving us a shot."

Lauren blinked back tears.

"Don't walk away from us."

"Jack, I need time to think." Her voice quavered. "Please let me go."

Dammit, he didn't want to give her the time to think. She would only relive her past and let it get in the way.

"Jack, please."

The tears she'd been holding back spilled onto her checks. He wanted to gather her in his arms and kiss them away. But the pleading look in her eyes made him release her. Pivoting on her heel, she hurried away.

Chapter 28

*A*fter arranging for a tow truck to take her car to the repair shop to get the graffiti removed and the tires replaced, Lauren spent the rest of the afternoon cleaning her unit. She scrubbed and washed until it shined like a diamond.

Usually she found cleaning helped clear her mind, but right now it wasn't working. Her head was still telling her she didn't need the added stress of Jack's drama, but her heart was yelling at her for being so stupid and walking away.

Lauren sent out an emergency call out to Ava and Jade. She hoped the girls could help with her problems. Ava suggested they meet up at Body Re-Sculpture; she had her eyes set on a very attractive personal trainer, and they could also let off steam on the gym equipment. Two birds, one stone.

Lauren agreed she could use a bit of physical therapy to help relieve the built-up tension.

Sweaty from a five-kilometer run on the treadmill, Lauren stretched out her tired limbs and filled Ava and Jade in on the events of the day, without giving away too many details of the time she'd spent with Jack. Their faces turned from happiness one moment to concern over the problem with Claire the next.

"Lauren, I've known you long enough to understand this thing with Jack is serious."

Jade's red, curly hair had broken free from her pony-tail and bounced around her flushed face.

Lauren stretched her arm out to the side. "Jade, you told me Jack doesn't do 'serious'."

"What would I know? I get my information from silly magazines. From what you've been telling us Jack isn't treating you like a one-night stand. He told you he *wants you*." Her stomached dropped. Would that be enough?

"Wanting is a lot different from love." The word *love* hit her like a bullet through the heart. Lauren bit her lip. What made her say love?

Jade's eyes lit up. "Do you *love* him?"

Did she? She couldn't compare her feelings for Jack with anything she'd ever experienced. She wanted to believe it had only been attraction, but she needed to get real and face what was so obviously staring right at her.

Yes, she loved Jack.

Over the last few weeks he'd shown her so many qual-ities she found more attractive than his sexy exterior. The afternoon she'd watched him train those beautiful kids at the football stadium was when she completely lost her heart to him. But her brain had needed extra time to catch up with her heart.

She nodded her answer, the lump in her throat making it difficult to speak.

"Oh, Lauren, that's wonderful." Jade gave her a sweaty hug.

Lauren shrugged her off. "Gross, Jade, no touchy-feely, you stink." She bent into a lunge to stretch out her calves. "I don't know if it is wonderful. It would be much easier if I didn't love him." Her heart raced at finally saying the words out loud.

After finishing her stretches, Jade sat cross-legged on the mat. "If you love the guy, give him a chance. He told you about the psycho bitch and the police are on to her."

"What if another psycho bitch turns up with a crazy story?"

"You can play the 'what if' game until the cows come home. You can play it safe, but you will never know if something great could come out of it. What do you have to lose?"

"My heart," Lauren whispered. "It nearly killed me trying to put it back together after Graham. It would be so much worse if Jack…" She couldn't say her fears out loud.

Jade sighed, and her shoulders sagged. "He's not Graham. You *know* that. He doesn't have a wife and kid hidden somewhere. Can you honestly say what you felt for Graham is anything like what you feel for Jack?" Lauren shook her head.

"You were young and living without love, he was good-looking, charming, and showered you with what you believed was love. It was totally understandable you fell for his deceit. But you're not that young, naïve girl anymore. You know better now."

"But Jack doesn't do relationships." Lauren's excuses, even to her own ears, sounded feeble.

"He wants one with you."

Lauren slumped on the mat next to Jade. "When did you become so smart?" She nudged her shoulder against Jade.

"I'm the wise one of the group. I thought you already knew that." Jade nudged Lauren back, then added with a serious tone, "Think about it carefully. Try not to be so quick to throw something away that could be really special. But if you do…" She gave Lauren an exaggerated wink. "Send him my way."

Lauren laughed. Jade could always put a smile on her face. This was who she called family. What would Lauren do without them?

Glancing over at Ava, who had been quiet during Lauren and Jade's deep and meaningful conversation, Jade asked, "Do you have anything to add?"

Ava was quick to give sex advice, but when it came to relationships she didn't believe they existed. She didn't do romantic dinners and long walks on the beach or anything that *sounded* like a relationship. "As long as my girl is getting mind-blowing sex there's nothing for me to say."

Ava showed no signs of having spent the hour exercising. Her hair hung sleek and neat, her makeup looked flawless, and her ultra-tight gym gear didn't have a trace of sweat.

Scrutinizing her own damp, knee-length tights and oversized blue t-shirt, Lauren touched her sweaty face and knew the minimal makeup she'd applied earlier had well and truly sweated off.

Lauren leaned back on her arms and frowned up at Ava. "I stink like a pig, and you look as fresh as a daisy. You're a freak, and I hate you."

Smiling sweetly, Ava stopped the treadmill and stepped off. "What's the matter, darlin'?

After all the wonderful sex you've had with Jack you'd think you'd be in a better mood."

Lauren ignored Ava's comment about wonderful sex with Jack, because if she thought about it too much she'd want to rush over to his house and jump him. She jabbed a finger in Ava's direction. "No one should look as good as you after a workout. You never have an ugly day! It's not fair, and I stand by what I said—you're a freak."

Stretching an arm out over her head, Ava bent her body to the side. "Keep having all that hot sex and you too will start glowing like the summer sun." Lauren scoffed.

Jade rolled her eyes.

Ava straightened, her attention focused on someone across the room. Her eyes turned seductive and a sly smile spread across her face. "It's time to get my summer glow. I'll see you later, ladies."

Lauren watched as Ava threaded her way through the

exercise equipment toward Craig, the extremely buff fitness trainer Ava had been flirting with during their last two visits.

"Poor guy," Jade said as she stretched her arm across her chest and watched Ava work her magic. "He's smitten with Ava and she's going to chew him up and spit him out. You know we're going to have to change gyms again." She blew out a frustrated breath. "I wish she'd stop sleeping with the trainers. I liked it here."

Lauren copied Jade's stretch and sighed. "Good thing we didn't buy a membership."

Chapter 29

It was six o'clock when Jack finished sorting through the box of paperwork which had been saved from Claire's destruction. He unpacked and put away the delivery of office supplies he had tried to convince Lauren he needed help with. Leaning back in the new, soft leather chair, he put his feet up on the shiny mahogany desk and admired the great job she'd done with the space. Amongst the office furniture and equipment, which she had styled with a warm and modern touch, were the more personal items that gave the room character.

She had a wall dedicated to football memorabilia and awards. His 2012 grand final winning jersey hung proudly next to his Australian captaincy one. He was glad he'd kept those in storage or Claire would have destroyed them too.

The adjacent wall was kept more personal. She'd displayed photos of different stages of construction of

Henderson's. She'd found photos of his father, wearing a hard hat, inspecting the site and talking to the builders. Another showed the grand opening of Henderson's Sports. His beaming father, with a full head of dark hair, stood proudly with his arm wrapped around his mother's shoulders. She looked exactly like Leah did now. His mother held Leah in her arms, and Jack stood shyly next to his father with his arm around the man's leg.

Lauren had included pictures from his first game of footy, no doubt provided by his mother, with his grubby uniform and skinned knees. His messy hair stood up in spikes, and his smile was huge as he sat on his father's shoulders. His mother stood close, her attention on her son's injured knees.

Jack's throat grew tight. Lauren never experienced the love of a real family, but she knew exactly what it should look like—she displayed it perfectly on his walls. She understood what family should be about but wouldn't reach out and grab it for herself.

With the office now finished she had no reason to keep coming back. Especially after the trouble Claire caused.

He thought he'd finally pushed through her insecurities. Thought he'd gotten her to trust again...trust him. But the mess with Claire had her running as fast as she could and once again building up walls and shutting him out.

Jack wanted to be the person she could turn to when times were hard, not someone who caused the trouble. He wanted to protect her from every Graham, Belinda, and Claire in the world.

His football lifestyle had once kept him from believing there could be such a thing as a strong, healthy relationship, but now, because of Lauren, he knew better. She had opened his eyes to the possibility of more.

He loved her.

Damn, he never thought he'd ever fall in love. In the past, the idea would have scared the hell out of him. But not anymore; not when Lauren's sweet, beautiful face came to mind.

She never would have opened up to him if she didn't feel something for him too. What did he need to do to convince Lauren to see they were great together and they were strong enough to cope with the drama Claire, or anyone else could bring?

Then it hit him. He may not be able to stop Claire on her rampage of destruction; could only hope the cops found her. Nor could he stop the tabloids from printing false stories about him. But there was one thing he could do to make Lauren's life easier. Deal with her money-hungry sister and give her one less problem in her life.

Dropping his feet from the desk, he opened his laptop. After a few clicks of the keyboard he found the information he needed. It was time to pay Belinda a visit.

Jack parked in front of Belinda's apartment block in the seediest part of Brimland Point. Old, run-down, red-brick apartments in need of repair lined the street. Graffiti was scrawled on the walls of the lower units, and the lawn was overgrown. Broken TVs, shredded lounges, and all sorts of debris lay in piles along the footpath.

Jack checked the dark surroundings, and for a moment, he considered leaving the death zone neighborhood. But he came there for a reason, and he wouldn't turn back now.

He got out of the car, careful not to step on something that could potentially kill him, and moved around a rusted bicycle with missing tires. He made his way up the cracked, uneven pathway that led to the dilapidated apartments. Thank God Belinda's apartment was situated on the ground floor. He didn't have to go inside the death trap.

He knocked on a graffiti-covered door and heard a TV blaring from somewhere beyond it. He hoped if Belinda was inside, she didn't leave him waiting too long. Thankfully, the door swung open before he had the chance to knock again.

A small, disheveled woman, with dirty blonde hair and clothes that had seen better days, stood in the doorway. A harsh frown appeared on her creased face. His fists clenched by his sides at the thought of Lauren having to deal with this mean-looking woman. When he finished with Belinda, Lauren would never have to see her again.

She squinted and trailed her bloodshot eyes up and down him. When recognition hit, her eyes widened and she smiled, showing stained, yellow teeth. "I know you."

She tucked a greasy strand of hair behind her ear,

puffed out her chest, and leaned her shoulder against the doorjamb. The seductive pose she tried to pull off made Jack's skin crawl.

There were no similarities between Lauren and Belinda except for the hazel color of their eyes, although Lauren's sparkled with health and happiness while Belinda's looked washed out and dull.

Belinda put a hand on her hip. If she thought anything about her was sexy, she was hugely mistaken. "You're Jack Henderson."

"Yes, I am. I want to talk to you about your sister Lauren." He got straight to the point, and her attempt at seduction dropped and turned to disgust. He preferred her hostility. The way she examined him a moment ago made him want to go home and take a long, hot shower.

"What's the bitch done now?" she spat.

His fingers curled tighter into fists. "We need to discuss the money situation you've got going on." He kept his voice cool and casual, which belied the rage boiling inside him.

"What's it got to do with you?" Her eyes narrowed. "Are you her new boy toy now? She has a thing for pretty, rich boys. You'll soon realize she's just a slut."

Jack had to gather a shitload of willpower to keep from wrapping his hands around her neck. Instead, he pulled out an envelope from the pocket of his jacket and handed it to her. "This is for you."

Belinda looked at it with suspicion. She opened the envelope and pulled out a wad of cash. Her eyes lit up like lights on a Christmas tree. "Holy shit!" she exclaimed, flicking through the hundred-dollar notes. With fast fingers, like she thought he would take it back, she stuffed the money back into the envelope and stored it down her top. "What's it for?"

His voice rumbled low and deep with warning. "You're going to leave Lauren alone, and you're never going to ask her for money again."

"How ya gonna stop me?" She scoffed.

Jack placed an arm on the doorframe, leaning forward. She stepped back, and her eyes widened with fright. All her bravado lost as she realized Jack was someone she couldn't mess with.

"Use the money I've given you wisely, because that's the last of it. You will no longer blackmail Lauren for more, and if you think for one moment that you can take her story and sell it to the media, you will deal with me, and I'll make your life a living hell." He casually slipped a hand in his jean pocket. "And you'll wish you had never met me."

Belinda sucked in a shaky breath. She wasn't dealing with Lauren anymore who she'd walked over for years. She was now playing with the big guys. Belinda wouldn't feel so big and tough anymore.

He straightened away from the door. "I'd like to say it was nice meeting you…" He shrugged and walked away.

The slamming of the door echoed out onto the dark street.

Chapter 30

---

*L*auren had gotten little sleep, her mind filled with thoughts of all that had happened over the last couple of days. Sleeping with Jack had been a huge step from breaking away from her past, but finally admitting she loved him had been earth-shattering. Her heart pounded at a rapid rate at admitting her love. But her heart and mind were at war, pulling her in two different directions. Her heart wanted her to take a chance, but her mind cautioned her about all the obstacles she'd have to face. Claire being a major one. Her skin turned cold at the thought of the vengeful woman.

It would've been so much easier if it had only been about sex with Jack. Walking away after the first time and never going back for more would have been the best thing to do. She scoffed. She didn't buy her own lie.

Walking into the kitchen, she put the coffee on. The smell of ground beans filled the space and she started to feel human again. When the coffee was done she poured herself a cup, then sat in the Lazy-Boy, curled her legs up under her, and sipped the extra-strong brew.

She wore the t-shirt Jack had given her the day she ripped her top at work. The soft fabric held a faint smell of woodsy cologne and Jack. She smiled, remembering the dark, hooded expression Jack wore when she modeled it for him the night they first made love. Memories of that sexy grin and his erotic caresses ran through her mind like an X-rated movie. She squirmed in the chair as heat simmered in her lower parts.

Jade and Ava wanted her to follow her heart and take the leap. Her palms grew sweaty at the thought. The thought of letting go and taking that step scared the living daylights out of her. She knew Jack cared for her, knew he wanted her, but how long would that last? He'd never wanted a committed relationship, so why would that change now? And if he were to commit, did she want to keep looking over her shoulder in case another woman came into their lives with more stories to tell? The problem with Belinda was big enough, could she then deal with Claire's revenge against Jack on top of that? Did she have the strength for more problems?

Lauren dressed, drove to work, and pulled into the space next to Jaime's car. The sky was gray, and she ran to her office, trying to avoid the light drizzle.

The last blackmail payment was due. Now that Jack's office was completed, she had the money to give to Belinda and hoped she would leave her alone for a while.

Calling out to Jaime, she let her know she was in the office then turned on the computer and waited for it to boot up. While she waited, her fingers trailed over her locket with Abby's hair tucked safely inside. But as she touch the warm metal and thought of Abby, the rush of pain that normally flooded her didn't hit with the usual force. An ache still pulled at her heart and sadness filled her, but it didn't cut so deep. Now her heart was filled with something else— something that helped her heal the pain she had felt for so many years. Her love for Jack.

After growing up with no affection, she believed she didn't deserve love. Her mother, Belinda, and even Graham helped seal tight that part of her heart. She'd sabotaged past relationships by dating men with no potential just so she wouldn't have to reopen it. But Jack blasted through the barrier, broke through the lock and pried it open again. She knew Jack deserved a chance. He was worth risking her heart over.

Hope for a future filled her with longing. She wanted to tell Jack she needed him in her life. She wanted to give them a chance.

But before she could go to him she needed to purge the demons of her own past and take care of Belinda first.

Jack's payment sat in her bank account and Lauren decided Belinda would never see any of it. She was fed up with being blackmailed. Blackmailed because she had once been young and naïve and put her trust in a slimy snake. Belinda could go to the media and spill the beans; she no longer cared. She'd had enough of keeping secrets. She was tired of living her life this way, tired of living with the 'what ifs'. Jack couldn't stop women like Claire trying to cause trouble, but she could stop herself from reacting to it. She didn't need to give them any of her time or energy.

It was time to live life for herself and not be dictated by others.

A burst of adrenaline kicked into her veins as she fished her phone out of her bag and dialed Belinda's number.

"What!" Belinda was never pleasant to talk to, but she sounded even more hostile than normal.

"Belinda, it's Lauren."

"Whadda ya want? I thought you had your big, hot shot boyfriend doin' your dirty work for you now?"

"What are you talking about?"

"Don't play dumb, you bitch. You sent your footy player boyfriend to my place to threaten me to leave you alone. Message received. I won't be callin' you again or sellin' your borin' as shit story. No one would give a shit about you anyway." Lauren heard the venom in Belinda's voice. "What did ya do to get his protection? No, wait… you just opened up your legs for him like the slut you are."

Lauren had heard enough to understand what was going on and couldn't stand to listen to Belinda for another minute. "Have a good life, Belinda."

She'd finally cut all ties. Relief lifted the weight of the world from her shoulders.

She disconnected the call with a smile. Jack had confronted Belinda, and now Lauren would never need to worry about her again. Even though Lauren promised to never give Belinda another cent, she knew her sister would have kept trying to blackmail her. But Jack fixed the problem for good. Exhilaration flooded her body, and she let out a giddy giggle.

If she had any doubts about her feelings for Jack before, they'd now been wiped away. Her heart burst with happiness. She needed to find him and thank him for what he'd done, but most importantly, she wanted to tell him how much she loved him.

Rushing to the doorway leading into the shop, she poked her head in to tell Jaime she needed to go out for a while. Jaime waved and told her she had everything under control. Picking up her bag from the desk, she raced out the back door.

Chapter 31

*L*auren rushed to her car with her head down, searching for her keys in her bag, when she bumped into someone.

Startled, she said, "Oh, sorry, I wasn't watching where I was going." She smiled and went to step around the woman she'd collided with.

The woman grabbed Lauren around the arm with a firm grip and pulled her to a stop. When Lauren turned back to tell the woman to remove her hands, recognition struck. This was the woman who had broken the candlesticks. The tiny hairs on the back of her neck rose. She hadn't had a good feeling about her that day and now unease stomped around like elephants in Lauren's stomach.

Before Lauren had the chance to speak, the woman sneered with a cruel expression.

"Don't walk away from me, bitch."

Lauren gritted her teeth and felt her blood bubble

hot. Totally fed up with people calling her a bitch, she shook her arm free. It throbbed where it had been held, and red finger marks were visible on her skin. It was going to bruise.

Lauren dug her hands into her hips. "What's your problem?"

The woman's lip curled in a hateful smile. "*You're* my problem. You think you can take what's mine?" Her gaze traveled up and down Lauren with disgust. "What the fuck does he see in you? You look as frigid as a nun."

"What are you talk…" Then it hit her. "Claire."

Concern replaced her annoyance. This was the person who'd trashed Jack's office and damaged her car, and by the crazed expression on her face, she didn't appear very stable. She needed to approach Claire carefully.

"So, you *do* know me," the woman said with a twisted smile.

The drizzle from earlier had gotten heavier. Claire pushed a lock of damp hair from her face, and it was then Lauren saw what Claire held in her hand. She sucked in her breath, and fear lodged in her throat. Claire held a very dangerous-looking silver knife. The woman was a little more than unstable, she was downright psychotic.

Lauren searched the carpark for help, but there was no one around. She took a couple of

small steps back toward her shop. Maybe if she got close enough she could make it inside and lock the door before Claire reached her.

If she kept Claire talking, hopefully she wouldn't notice Lauren moving away. "Jack mentioned you."

"Did he *mention* that he panted after me in the office like a dog in heat until I let him fuck me on his desk?" Claire's dark hair hung like damp curtains around her face and mascara dripped down her cheeks, giving her an even more disturbing appearance.

Lauren shook her head. "No." Her voice sounded like a strangled whisper as she remembered Claire's handiwork on Jack's desk with a sharp object, probably with the knife she now held.

"Well, he did. He wanted me. He said he couldn't live without me. Did he *mention* that?" Her voice rose with each word as she paced in front of Lauren, waving the knife at her face.

"And now you're in my way."

Lauren took two more small steps back. She wasn't dealing with an angry ex-girlfriend, she was dealing with someone who was mentally unstable. Lauren needed to try and calm her down. "Claire, I know you're upset. I don't blame you for being angry." She needed to try to get her to believe she was on her side. "Let's go inside and out of the rain. I'll make you a coffee and we can talk." Not that she had any intention of letting her inside. As soon as Lauren got to the office she'd lock the door before Claire entered and call the police.

She slowly started to turn around, praying that putting her back toward Claire and the knife wouldn't be a bad idea. But before she could take a step farther Claire grabbed her by the arm and swung her around.

"I don't want your fucking coffee. I want you to leave Jack the hell alone. He's mine! You're so prissy I bet you screw like a virgin. Did Jack tell you how he said I was the best fuck of his life? You don't deserve a man like Jack."

Lauren knew Claire was trying to rattle her, and at any other time, it would have worked. She would've walked away from this woman, promising to never see Jack again. The problems he came with were not worth her time or energy. But her feelings for Jack had changed, and she now knew he was worth everything. She wanted to fight for him and take the good with the bad.

It was up to her to grab hold of what she wanted and not let go and damn anyone who tried to stop her. She'd gotten Belinda out of her life and now Claire needed to go. Something snapped inside her and anger consumed her, and she forgot about the knife in Claire's hand.

Lauren pulled her shoulders back and tilted her chin up. "Jack's not yours and never will be."

Claire's eyes widened, and her face turned a deep red.

"If you weren't trashing things and being a pain in his ass, you'd be long forgotten by now."

Claire sucked in a breath and made a choking sound. Lauren knew she was taking a risk speaking to her like this, but she couldn't stop herself. Years of built-up frustration at being told what to do came pouring out.

"He cares for me. Not you—me," Lauren said, placing a hand on her chest. "Actually, he loves me." She wasn't sure he did, but Claire didn't know any better. "And I love him. So you need to get over this crazy obsession you have with Jack and move on."

"No!" Claire screamed hysterically and held the knife in front of Lauren's face. "He loves me!"

Lauren stumbled a couple of steps away from the knife. She took a deep, shaky breath, trying to stay as calm as she could with a sharp-looking blade inches from her face. "Claire, I'm sorry I upset you. Come inside, and we can sit down and talk. We're getting soaked in the rain." Claire tugged at her dripping hair. "Do you think I give a shit if you're getting wet?

Leave Jack alone or I'll carve up your pretty face." And she swung the knife toward Lauren. Lauren's reflexes kicked in and she automatically lifted her arm to ward off the blow. She waited for the searing burn of the blade to slice through her skin, but the pain never came.

Instead of the knife slicing through Lauren's skin, her forearm collided with Claire's wrist and knocked the blade out of her hand, sending it clattering to the concrete.

Claire scrambled down on her hands and knees, but before she could crawl to it, Lauren kicked it out of her reach. Claire rose and went to follow the knife just as a car pulled into the carpark with screeching tires.

Jack bounded out of the car and raced toward them.

Chapter 32

_J_ack saw Claire's wild, panicked eyes dart around, looking for an escape. But before she could take another step, Jack was on her. He grabbed her arms and held them tight behind her back. Screaming, she kicked at him and tried to break free, but he kept a firm grip. There was no way he was about to let her go.

Running his gaze over Lauren's wet body, he couldn't see any blood but asked just in case he'd missed something. "Lauren, are you hurt?" She shook her pale face.

Waves of relief washed over him. "Call the police."

Her eyes widened like her brain had once again clicked on to what was happening, and she dug around her bag for her phone, spilling most of the contents on the ground in her rush.

Her hands shook as she dialed triple zero. He wanted to hold her and comfort her instead of holding onto the enraged woman in his arms.

The call had barely been made when a police car pulled up behind Jack's car. Two officers ran toward Jack and took Claire out of his hands.

Jack and Lauren ran toward each other. Jack opened his arms and Lauren ran into them. Brushing back her wet hair, he cupped her cheeks and placed urgent kisses over her face. He put his hands on her shoulders, pushed her at arm's length, and scanned her body from head to toe, needing to see for himself she hadn't been hurt.

"Are you all right?" he asked, then ran his hands over her, looking for injuries.

Stopping his hands, Lauren held them to her chest and kissed him. "I'm okay. Claire didn't hurt me." A shudder shook through her body underneath his palm, or it could have been him vibrating through her.

Jack pulled her to his chest in a tight embrace. "But she could have hurt you. God, if she did, I never could have lived with myself. When I saw that knife..." He shook his head then placed his forehead against hers.

"I'm okay," she whispered.

All he could think to do to reassure himself she really was okay was to kiss her with everything in his heart.

When the kiss broke they stood gazing at each other. Their emotions and feelings laid out bare for one another. Jack's heart raced with excitement. What he saw in Lauren's eyes reflected what he knew shone from his own.

The sound of a car door slamming broke their connection, and they turned toward the police officers.

"How did the police get here so quickly?" Lauren asked.

Jack shrugged.

"I called them."

They both turned to find Jaime standing at the back-door of the shop, twisting her hands together.

"I came into your office to get Mrs. Sherman's order, and I saw that woman…" She pointed to Claire. They could hear Claire screaming from inside the police car. "…grab your arm, and I saw the knife in her hand. I called triple zero, and they told me to stay inside." She looked at Lauren with tear-soaked eyes. "I wanted to come out and help you…" Her voice cracked.

Lauren rushed over and hugged her. "You did the right thing. The police came just in time. Thank you."

The police officers had plenty of questions and asked Lauren, Jack, and Jaime to come down to the police station to give an official statement. Lauren agreed to go right away, saying she wanted to get it over with.

Chapter 33

Later that day, Lauren sat curled up in Jack's lap on his couch, enjoying his fingers running through her hair. The crazy events of the day ran through her mind. Finally standing up to Belinda was like having shackles removed from her wrists. She was now free from the blackmailing. The relief pouring through her made her light-headed.

Claire wanting to hurt her had been the scariest experience of her life. How she found the courage to stand up to her she'd never know. The police had informed them that Claire had been in and out of McMahon's Mental Health Clinic for the past two years. During her recent stay she'd left without being discharged by doctors, and her family had been looking for her ever since. Lauren inwardly shook; she didn't want to think about how close to getting hurt, or worse, she'd gotten. She hoped Claire's family could get her the help she needed.

Lauren should've been exhausted from the adrenaline

shock of the day's events, but she didn't want to sleep. She wanted to spend every moment she could with Jack. He'd really come through for her, in more ways than one.

"Belinda isn't going to ask me for any more money."

Jack's fingers stilled for a beat then continued stroking her hair.

"I called her earlier today to tell her she wasn't getting any more from me no matter what she threatened to do."

Jack kissed the top of her head. "Good for you." The vibrations from his deep voice rumbled through her body as she leaned against his chest.

"But you beat me to it." She tilted her head back so she could see his face. He cupped her chin in his strong hands while his thumb caressed her jaw. "Why did you do it?"

Leaning forward, he placed a gentle kiss on her lips. "I did it because I hated seeing you treated that way." Giving her lips another kiss, he added, "I also did it because I love you."

Lauren's breath hitched, and she sat up to get a better look at him. Jack must have thought she was going to pull away because he wrapped his arms around her, pulled her closer, and secured her on his lap.

"I know you have a hard time trusting. Your experience is enough to make anyone have major doubts, but please trust me when I tell you there's nothing on this earth I want more than you. All the money and fame in the world could go tomorrow, dammit, I'd make it go away if that's what you wanted just so I can have you. I never thought I'd ever feel this way. Never saw myself spending forever with anyone. Now all I see is you. There is no forever if I don't have you." His eyes pleaded with her to believe him. "Lauren, I *love* you."

Tears welled and blurred her vision. She blinked and hot rivers ran down her cheeks.

"Please tell me those are good tears," Jack said, kissing them from her face.

Lauren nodded. The lump in her throat prevented her from speaking.

After a moment, she took a deep breath and hoped her voice didn't waver. "When I ran into Claire I was on my way to see you."

She gazed at his gorgeous face, seeing beyond the pretty façade to the man who truly loved her. A man who was generous and kind, someone who loved her enough to want to protect her from the madness she'd endured all these years.

"Before I called Belinda to tell her she wasn't getting any more money, I finally woke up and saw the man you are. I kept judging you for something someone else did, and I know how unfair that was. Your heart is huge, and I can see you're loyal and loving to those who are important to you. I finally saw *you*. I realized people like Belinda and Claire didn't matter as long as I had you. I'm one of those people in your life you want to love and protect and I see it now." She picked up Jack's hand and placed it on her racing heart. "I was coming to tell you how I felt. I wanted to tell you I loved you."

Jack blew out a long breath, like he'd been waiting a long time to hear the words. He pushed her hair back from her face, brushed the tears from her cheeks, and met her gaze. His love for her and their future together shone from the emerald depths. How could she have run from this man? And then he kissed her so passionately it caused her toes to curl, and she knew there'd be no more running.

As he tunneled his fingers through her hair, his tongue swept inside her mouth, and she let out a soft sigh of pleasure. She could make out with the super-sexy sports star every day of her life. Life was good!

Jack scooped her off his lap and into his arms as he rose from the sofa. Linking her arms around his broad shoulders, Lauren nuzzled the warm, soft skin at his neck as he carried her into the bedroom.

He smacked a kiss on her lips and beamed, "I'm the luckiest *Mr. Pretty* in the world!"

Epilogue

Colors exploded and danced in the sky above Lauren and Jack as they sat on a picnic blanket on top of a grassy hill. They laughed, kissed, and made ridiculous New Year promises they knew they would never keep as the summer breeze, still warm at midnight, whistled around them.

Lauren gazed at the sleeping bundle in her arms. No colors in the sky were as beautiful as the miracle she held. Lauren and Jack had been blessed with a baby boy born on Christmas Day, their precious Christmas miracle and the love of their lives. Lauren never thought she could be any happier as she leaned against the warmth of her husband's chest.

Bending his head, Jack kissed her shoulder. "Happy New Year, Mrs. Henderson." Turning her head, she kissed Jack on the side of his jaw.

Then both their attention went to their sleeping baby.

Lauren kissed his head covered with soft brown hair, and Jack stroked a finger along his delicate hand.

Jack shifted and Lauren felt him move away. Turning, she watched as he pulled out a small box he'd hidden in the nappy bag and held it out toward her.

She glanced at the box and then at Jack. "What's this?"

Chuckling, he said, "Open it and find out."

Adjusting the baby in her arm, she lifted the leather lid of the box with her free hand. A silver locket with a swirled pattern made from diamonds sat on plush black velvet. She gasped with surprise, and her hand automatically reached for the cheap, tarnished one around her neck.

"It's beautiful."

"I thought you could put Ryan's hair on one side and Abby's on the other," he said. A tear slid down her check, and Jack wiped it with his thumb. "You don't have to replace it with yours if you don't want to. I just thought a new one might be nice to keep both their hair in it. But I've upset you, I'm sorry, I made a mistake."

Jack went to put the box away, but she placed a hand over his, stopping him. "I love it. It's a perfect idea." She smiled.

"Then why the tears?"

"I'm hormonal, everything makes me cry." She laughed. "And I'm happy and so in love with you and Ryan. This gift is beautiful. Thank you." She leaned over to give him a kiss. Ryan made a snorting sound in his sleep and they broke apart laughing.

The crowd around them cheered into the midnight summer breeze.

"Happy New Year, Mr. Pretty."

About Sonia Stanizzo

Sonia Stanizzo is a contemporary romance author living in the beautiful south coast of New South Wales, Australia with her husband and three children. When she's not dreaming up stories about couples and their road to finding love, sometimes bumpy but always a lot of fun, she can be found taking pole dancing lessons, reading and writing.

Thank you so much for reading The Trouble with Mr. Pretty. I hope you enjoyed meeting Jack and Lauren and loved them as much as I do.

www.soniastanizzo.com

soniastanizzo@gmail.com

Visit my website to join my reader newsletter for free books, new releases and giveaways. Come and say hello on social media:

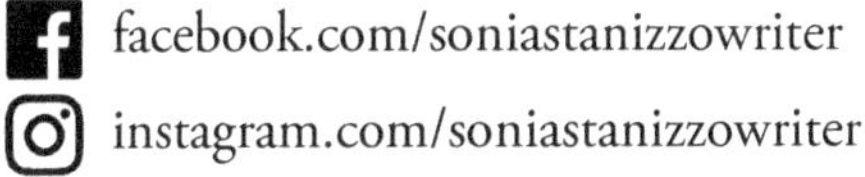

www.ingramcontent.com/pod-product-compliance
Lightning Source LLC
Chambersburg PA
CBHW070547120726
47909CB00007B/2272